The OutBreak

By Lee David Congerton

The OutBreak Hotel

First Published 2022
Theoutbreakhotel@wordpress.com
Facebook: The OutBreak Hotel
Twitter @HotelOutbreak
Instagram: Lee David Congerton

To Emma, you are the Anton Ego to my chef Gusto. Hopefully, I have prepared something to your liking.

- Love Lee

"Christ promised a resurrection of the dead, I just thought he had something a little different in mind." — Hershel Greene.

Chapter List

Prologue

The apocalypse is all panic and no disco.

In other words, it is really, really rubbish. It's the very similar feeling, you get when opening a tin of Quality Street chocolates, only to find your Nan's sewing kit sort of rubbish. Did I mention that it's really rubbish?

Occurring on a Sunday of all days which annoyed most people to no end. After all, if it did have to happen, then at the very least could it not have happened on a Monday morning? Thus, saving millions of people from an angry, slow-moving commute.

But the end of the world had no regard for anybody's weekend plans and was officially declared Black Sunday at precisely 3pm GMT. This wasn't an intended slight on the original Black Sunday of April 1935, but just a lack of imagination by the media at the time. Personally, I would have gone with Z-day myself, seeing as the dead were coming back to life with a ravenous appetite. It's crazy right? Actual zombies running around, causing all sorts of mayhem. Just like a George A. Romero movie.

At first it was all very confusing, as the government politely asked the general public to stay at home and wear a mask where possible for their own safety. But this seemed to make everyone very angry indeed, especially when it was discovered several raves had been held at number ten Downing Street during this time. Who knew the prime minister was such a party animal!

Next it was all a bit shouty and even a bit rioty as people decided they would prefer to gather in mass and go to the beach. This in turn was followed by running and screaming, lots and lots of screaming.

According to the word on the street and by street, I mean various tweets and memes. This was all the result of a secret underground lab in Wuhan China, full of genetically created abominations. Other people would have you believe, it was caused by some very disgruntled monkeys who had stolen altered DNA samples in India. Then there were the extreme conspiracy theory nuts, a small but vocal group who were convinced this was the result of 5G phone tower side effects. All of which had been orchestrated by none other than Microsoft Mogul, Bill Gates.

But my personal favourite theory related all the way back to 1962 Tanzania, where an epidemic of laughing had broken out, lasting almost a full year. Several thousand people had been affected, across several villages. In fact, it had gotten so bad that a school was forced to close. It wasn't all smiles and good times though, as this led to crying, fainting, rashes, severe pain, madness and the odd case of cannibalism.

Personally, the one thing I knew for sure, was that I happened to be on the series finale of the Tiger King when Black Sunday was declared. Did Joe Exotic get out of Prison? Did Carole Baskin go to prison for allegedly turning her ex-husband into tiger chow? These are the questions that keep me up late at night, well that and the sound of bloated zombie flesh beating against the doors.

Honestly a few billion people come back from the dead and it's all panic this and mass hysteria that. There just wasn't any regards for a man's Netflix playlist anymore, but I digress.

In the weeks leading up to Black Sunday there had been a rather loud bang from a lab up somewhere in the northeast region of England, which in turn was promptly followed with denial from people in very nice suits. Next came false reassurances and daily updates on the ever-present situation, with instructions for everyone to always remain two meters apart, just out of chomping distance.

But alas, the allure of the seaside proved too much for the unusually sunny time of the year as people took the new rules with a pinch of salt. Which ultimately led to little Derek from down the road contracting the virus and soon having an overwhelming urge to munch on his family's vital organs.

But that was all so long ago, that it seems silly to get all hung up on the who, where and why of it all at this point.

Those that did manage to survive adapted to the new order of things, soon learning there was a ten-minute grace period before any of the bitten come back and try to eat your face off. Which is plenty of time to fold the washing, make a sandwich and grab a blunt instrument to bash their little zombie brains in. Admittedly it is best to make haste if they are in gatherings as it can be extremely difficult to get the timings right. Usually, they just pop back up like an evil game of whack-a-mole, minus winning any tickets to use at an arcade prize booth.

And then there's the infected birds, which if you're not careful can swoop down in the blink of an eye and rip chunks of flesh from you in an instant. The equivalent of a zombie drone strike I suppose. Luckily, these days most of the feathered fiends have all but rotted away, but even so, it is best to keep one eye skywards, just in case.

Personally, I have become rather adapt to this new, cruel and desolate world. Thriving far better now than I ever had ever working the Monday to Friday lifestyle. Yes, having your loved one's innards munched on is hardly everyone's cup of tea it is fair to admit. But for me it was a welcome and much needed change of pace. As a matter of fact, I had been social distancing long before it was the cool thing to do. #Trendsetter as the kids would say, or at least they would if their vocal cords hadn't turned to mush.

Apologies, I haven't introduced myself now have I? After all the end of the world is no excuse for poor manners.

I'm The Manager, self-appointed owner and operator of the finest destination this side of the apocalypse.

Welcome to your new home, the fabulous Holiday Inn Express, Stevenage.

Do enjoy your stay.

The Manager

Isolation can be good for the soul, providing you ignore the crippling loneliness and the longing for the warmth of another human being that is. But it is how the man who would become The Manager survived on a daily basis. Having never left his hometown of Stevenage when the world started to fall apart around him. Deciding it best to stay put in his overly expensive and poorly maintained rented house. Unfortunately, his next-door neighbours, who were unbearable enough at the best of times let alone when the dead walked the earth, had also decided to remain at home until things blew over. But three months on from Black Sunday things were very far from over.

Spurred on by a newfound level of hunger there was no putting it off any longer, now was the time to venture outside. He hatched a plan, quite a brave one it might be said, to drive his beat-up car towards the industrial area of town in search of supplies. If successful, he could set up camp at Costco's, an Americanised wholesaler that sold just about everything that fit onto a robust pallet.

With the possibility of mounds of sealed food, clothes, beds and tools, it was a zombie survivalists dream! It also came along with the bonus of being his former place of work, so armed with intimate knowledge of the building it was worth the risk. Although it hadn't been a Costco when he worked there previously. Instead, it was home to a John Lewis warehouse that had been leased out to store equipment for the 2012 London Olympic Games.

That was one of his more memorable jobs over the years, having been his role to inspect all manner of things ranging from folding chairs to official gold torches. Once everything had been given his stamp of approval, it was all carefully prepared and sent off to the various venues ready for the big event. He had been a small but vital cog in a proud time in British history, even if no one knew it. Those were some good times indeed and he was sad to see it all come to an end. But in hindsight perhaps a gold torch signed by David

Beckham wouldn't have been as useful as say sixty pallets of tinned spaghetti bolognaise given the current climate.

He stood behind thick, blackout bedroom curtains and peered outside, careful not to catch any unwanted attention before slowly drawing them back. From here he could inspect the surrounding area. No moving cars, no people idly going about their daily lives and more to the point, no gatherings of the undead to be seen anywhere. The sky was a clear blue, dotted with the occasional white cloud which was only a couple of shades lighter than his own pale skin. Clearly being trapped inside wasn't giving him the required amount of vitamin D.

On the plus side, pollution had all but cleared up at an amazing rate thanks to the pandemic, displaying the resiliency of mother nature. Flowers bloomed, bees returned, the oceans became clearer, dolphins even swam the canals of Venice. In fact, apart from the odd crisp packet tumble weeding down the street and a couple of wheelie bins that had toppled over, it all looked rather tranquil. But there was a storm on the horizon, one that no one could possibly escape. Without people to run pumps that divert rainfall and rising groundwater, the subways of huge sprawling cities like London had flooded within hours of Black Sunday.

Lacking human oversight, glitches in oil refineries and nuclear plants went unchecked, resulting in massive fires, nuclear explosions and devastating nuclear fallout. Also, in the wake of humanities demise, mountains of waste were left behind, much of it plastic, which would likely persist for thousands of years.

But on this street, in this moment in time, it all looked perfectly serene, he couldn't let that fool him though. In every shadow lurked ravenous potential danger, not to mention what could be hiding overhead in tree branches and on rooftops, poised to launch an all-out assault.

Readying himself for the perilous journey across town, he tied his shoes, put on his favourite grey hoodie and grabbed his car keys. Normally he would never have left the house without thoroughly checking his hair and brushing his teeth. But the last of the hair gel had long since been used and the last of the toothpaste ran out eight days prior. To say his breath was atrocious would have been a massive understatement, it hung in the air like the stench of sour milk and if downwind would alert the dead to his location with pinpoint accuracy.

There was an old Roman trick he had heard of, that urine could be used to clean and whiten teeth. But after trying it for a couple of days, he decided urine was a poor substitute for minty fresh breath.

Leaving his home for the first time in three months he poked his head out the front door like a meerkat checking for danger. It appeared to be all quiet on the western front as he took his first steps into the unknown. The weighty door clicking shut behind him with a sense of unease. Oddly the first thing he noticed was that somebody had stolen his doormat, which wasn't even particularly a nice one. Yet someone had gone to the time and effort to steal it during the three months he was held up, which annoyed him far more than it should have.

The street was ghost quiet, usually the area would have been filled with chattering mums and the clatter of plastic buggy wheels taking their children to and from the nearby school. But there was only a terrible silence, an unnatural stillness that caused his heart to beat a little faster.

Cautiously he took the short walk across the weed strewn garden path towards his car which was parked on the road opposite. Thankfully, no one had stolen that, probably as they couldn't get it to start. It was a 2008 Dodge Avenger, which according to Auto Trader while unique and sporty looking, is still a budget car at mainstream prices, with cheap, ugly interior, and dull to drive. Still, it did the job, most of the time.

The Dodge had started to accumulate a horrid green scum along the edge of the windows which he found most unsettling, as this was his pride and joy. Usually, he would take it to be hand cleaned once a month, but the car wash was now long dormant, and zombies would make for poor valets.

This wasn't just a car to him, this was a sleek machine built for speed and endurance, one of the rare Dodge Avengers to drive along

British roads. He loved and cherished this car like it was the child he never had.

Just a few months ago when the world was normal, he made the mistake of telling a work colleague that he called his car Florence, after the band Florence and the Machine whose style of music had been described as dark, robust and romantic, much like his beloved car. But his former colleague was quick to inform him the car was the machine part of the band, which would make him Florence. Luckily, the apocalypse caused that nickname to die out rather quickly.

With a firm push of the key-fob, the doors unlocked with an awkward clunk, he opened the driver's side door as a wave of stale air filled his senses causing an unpleasant tickle in the back of his throat. He stifled a cough, not wanting to cause any unnecessary noise which only made the urge to cough even worse. Placing his hands over his mouth was just enough to muffle the sound from any nearby undead ears.

Inside was exactly how he left it three months prior, a work bag hastily slung onto the back seat containing now obsolete paperwork and half a bottle of stale, strawberry flavoured water. There was a work phone in the back footwell which had long since ran out of battery. Sadly, unbeknownst to him the last phone call was from a woman called Katie, whom he used to work with. Her voice now captured for all time in a voicemail that could never be retrieved. She had called to say she always liked him in more than a professional capacity and asked him to run away with her to the Isle of Wight, where it was meant to be safe.

Sadly, Katie never did make it to the Isle of Wight.

Having seen one too many horror movies, he checked the backseat for any unwanted guests, but besides a single garden variety spider it was all clear. The spider had set up residency here, creating an impressive, intricate web, which was easily destroyed with a single swipe.

The Dodge may have been his pride and joy, but it was far from perfect as it constantly needed maintenance. It was far from the sleek and enduring machine he thought it to be, as periodically it would break down, leaving him stranded at the side of the motorway, but still he loved it regardless. After all, we all have our little flaws.

However, one of its biggest flaws was that it didn't even have a working radio, instead he used to substitute it with Spotify on his phone. Improvise, adapt and overcome as Bear Grills used to say. He missed music more than people at this stage, longing for an upbeat song from his favourite decade of the nineteen-eighties. But perhaps blaring out a cover of Wild Thing from 1984 wasn't the best idea right now.

Placing the key into the ignition, which was oddly placed on the left-hand side of the steering wheel, he gave it a turn. Nothing happened, not even a squeak of life, as unbeknownst to him, his next-door neighbours had tampered with the mighty Dodge, syphoning petrol from the tank a week prior. They had managed to take just about every drop, except for the petrol that sat within the engine block itself. He turned the key again as the Dodge let out a pathetic, high-pitched whine, like a child refusing to get out of bed.

"Come on, come on Florence" he said whilst firmly gripping the wheel. "I'm sorry I left you all alone out here, how about a fresh coat of wax once we get where we're going?"

He turned the key once more as suddenly the engine roared into life, accepting his offer. Not wanting the engine to give out, he put his foot down on the accelerator and together they zoomed down the street at almost dangerous speeds. Zipping in and out of abandoned cars that littered the road, narrowly missing a large white van as the Dodge managed to get a full half a mile down the road before it spluttered, juddered and coughed a final dying breath.

"Well now you only get half a coat of wax!" he said annoyed, turning the key back and forth in vain.

The Dodge died in one of the many evacuated zones meaning any undead brutes were few and far between. Shortly after Black Sunday the military had rolled through town, going door to door to save as many people as possible. The problem was that no one knew exactly where they were being evacuated to, for all he knew it could have been somewhere even worse. So, against all advice he decided to take his chances at home, besides, he couldn't leave the Dodge.

But any undead stragglers that remained in the evac zones were even more hostile due to the lack of food, as quite frankly a hangry zombie was a dangerous zombie. Once resurrected, Zombies tended to go one of two ways with their behaviour. The first being to seek out others like them, thus creating a gathering, which could range in numbers from just a handful to several hundred. While others became fiercely territorial, these ones marking out their territory with bile and a horrid discharge from their anal glands much like animals. Some would even let out a terrifying roar, stating they were not to be trifled with. Luckily, the streets appeared to be clear of mass gatherings and anal discharges.

A few more desperate turns of the ignition accompanied by several four-letter expletive pleas later, the mighty Dodge had officially given up the ghost. In the unlikely event there was an Uber just around the corner, the rest of the journey would have to be made on foot. There wasn't really much half a mile down the road from his home, mostly just abandoned and raided houses and various footpaths that led to local woodlands. These contained nothing more than the occasional well decorated, hidden stone and the odd rotting corpse.

Needing an alternative automatic car with exceptional boot space and ideally some go faster stripes, he left the Dodge in the middle of a street and said his farewells. "I will come back for you, as soon as I can" he said, as a singular tear rolled down his cheek, as if mourning the loss of an old friend.

Now exposed to the elements and failing to have the foresight to grab a weapon of sorts to defend himself with, he contemplated heading back home. But given the lack of food and mired with urine fresh breath it wasn't a difficult decision to push onwards, soon finding himself walking through the woods leading to the outskirts of the town centre.

This area of Stevenage was known as Monks Wood, where the figure of a headless monk was said to have haunted. In fact, going as far back as 1974, an eleven-year-old boy gave an account convincing enough that police saw fit to search the woods. Of course, it turned out to be nothing more than a child's active imagination. Ironically when the dead really did start to rise, it was all just dismissed as an elaborate hoax. In hindsight a headless monk would have been much more pleasant to deal with, at least he couldn't bite you.

The journey on foot wouldn't take too long, half an hour or so at the most assuming there wasn't any trouble along the way. He set off at an urgent pace, placing his hands in his hoodie pockets, pulling out a light blue medical face mask. "Oh yeah, I forgot they made us wear these things all the time" he chuckled to himself "for all the good they did." In retrospect perhaps wearing masks had been a blessing in disguise, pre-muzzling a potential zombie, giving any would be meals a chance to escape.

The sunlight pierced the thick canopy of trees as twisted shadows danced in front of him along the beaten path. The trees swayed gently with the cool breeze, creaking ever so slightly as they did so. In here you would have had no idea that the world was in such disarray. Several fluffy grey squirrels scurried up and down trees as he stopped for a moment to watch them, it was all so picturesque. That was until he absentmindedly stepped into a thick brown, gooey puddle that was the remains of someone's lower torso.

Even out in the open there was no avoiding the rancid smell of the disturbed body. This was the first time he had seen a dead body up close; films didn't really do the vileness justice. It was bloated and badly gnawed by wild animals. He should have been freaked out, but the truth was that it barely looked human anymore, in any case the smell made him quickly move along.

Emerging from a clearing he dragged his shoe through the long grass, wiping off the thick brown muck and was greeted by the sight of the local Asda supermarket. The supermarket was now just an empty shell as people had taken what they deemed to be the essentials for surviving. Which in most cases turned out to be ninety-four packs of toilet roll, which while useful, didn't taste great.

Now all that remained here were two rather dapper, suit clad zombies, stumbling around the empty car park. Somehow, they had managed to overturn a shopping trolley, trapping a seagull which was frantically squawking at its assailants. Their attention was solely focused on the infected fowl, as the beasts snapped and snarled at the helpless bird. Their hands too fat and bloated to fit through the metal bars, which seemed to frustrate them to no end. Eventually they would get a hold of the bird or it would escape their vile clutches, either way they hadn't noticed a human shaped buffet sneak past.

The next stop on his journey, was the town centre itself. If Stevenage is famous for anything, besides its several hundred roundabouts,' it's that the entire town was built with cyclists in mind. Boasting cycle paths adjacent to almost every main road, combined with accompanying underpasses. But despite these dedicated paths, cyclists had always insisted on using the roads beside them, proving that as a species we were always doomed.

Born and raised in Stevenage, or as it was once pronounced on BBC news "St' Evan-age" he knew all the best routes to take, allowing to travel with extra stealth. Using every back alley and underpass, he soon found himself undetected in the heart of the town, purpose built for pedestrian traffic. There wouldn't be any cars here, but it did lead straight to the multi-story car park, a mere five-minute walk away. This was more than likely his best bet.

The town centre had been well known for its wide assortment of shops, which included but were not limited to; Starbucks, Costa coffee, Cupps coffee shop, The Mad hatter café and Esquires coffee. It's just a shame he didn't really care for coffee all that much.

Just about every shop had been ravaged to the point of being almost unrecognisable with all manner of debris covering the ground like a dirty blanket. Windows had been smashed, fixtures ripped out and a gooey, reddish-brown substance was on just about every surface. There was a smell that lingered in the air, like rusted iron which overwhelmed the senses, bringing with it a heavy sense of dread.

He knew roughly three months had passed since Black Sunday, but there was no real way to tell how much time had passed. Time is a funny concept when it comes to the end of the world, which day of the week it was, was no longer relevant. Each day was simply judged by what the weather was like and more importantly if there was anything close by that wanted to eat you.

There seemed to be none of the latter on this day besides the previous dapper zombies and the weather was still rather pleasant. Sunny but not too hot for his fair complexion, just coming up to summer to hazard a guess. The ground crunched underfoot which seemed to echo around for miles, possibly alerting anyone or thing to his presence. It was like walking on a thick carpet of corn flakes, each step louder than the last.

In a moment of self-doubt and suddenly feeling very exposed, a primal instinct to retreat to the safety of home kicked in. Technically he was still renting that house and if indeed three months had passed then he would owe a total of £2400 in back rent. Not to mention council tax and water rates etc. If one day the world was to be restored to its former self, the potential debt would be most severe indeed. Just the thought of his current credit score made him shudder with horror.

Until now, the furthest he had dared venture was into the back garden, which was only to relieve his bowels before locking himself back within the safety of those four walls. The last time he visited the town centre was a mere two days before everything went into lockdown mode, stocking up enough food and water to keep going once rationed properly. The usual rule of never go shopping on an empty stomach wasn't an option today.

But still, it was nice just to be out of the house, especially away from the noisy neighbours. Each night the paper-thin walls would allow him to hear their deep and meaningful conversations which mostly involved yelling at each other and smashing things. It was only a matter of time until they attracted the wrong kind of attention, of the bitey variety.

Having reached the fountain in the middle of town which had turned a lovely shade of lime green, not too dissimilar from the edges of the Dodge windows he was faced with two options. The first being to keep pushing onwards to the multi-story car park, hoping there was a car well suited for his needs. The second was to get out of sight and head into the nearest building, which in this case was the clothing store, Primark.

There was a certain amount of appeal in option two as some clean clothes would have done nicely right about now. There are only so many times a man can turn his boxershorts inside out and back to front before they lose that fresh feeling. After that he could look in the versatile retail store Wilko for any potential pick 'n' mix sweets for the rest of the journey.

Quickly reasoning with himself that option two was worth the risk and perhaps there would be enough time to swing past the local library and pick up a book on hot-wiring cars for dummies. But seeing as he didn't have his library card on him, perhaps not.

The automatic doors to Primark had long since lost their power, one of the push doors was off its hinges and jammed in at a peculiar angle. Crouching underneath and into the store, it took him a moment to gather his bearings. Light streamed in through broken windows, reflecting off the thousands of scattered glass shards like an apocalyptic disco ball. Clearly, he wasn't the first person to come here as it was an awful mess, somewhat resembling the aftermath of a black Friday sale. There was a surprising amount of clothing left behind amongst the destruction, much of it still neatly folded on the shelves. Whomever had been here before wasn't interested in looting, but more so in causing damage to the long-standing store.

Women's clothing and accessories were placed on the ground floor, whilst; the upper floor was men's wear and children's apparel. It was just about light enough to see into certain areas but there was no telling what may lurk in the shadows towards the back of the store, so he decided to give that area a wide birth. A discarded metal railing caught his eye, which he immediately picked up as a means of protection and slowly crept forwards, ever mindful of each step. Realistically he knew there was a far greater chance of hurting himself with the railing than actually hitting a zombie. It was fair to say that hand eye coordination wasn't his strongest suit.

He previously thought that should the day come that the dead walked the earth, he would have been more than ready for the situation. Having once been an avid fan of the Walking dead TV show but gave up towards the later seasons as it had become a bit too bleak for his taste. The irony of the situation was not lost on him.

In the Walking dead they tended to ask three questions to any newcomers to the group: How many walkers have you killed? How many people have you killed? And finally, why?

It was highly unlikely that none, none and I was too busy eating jars of Nutella whilst cowering under my duvet would have been acceptable answers to join the group.

He went up the motionless escalator and around the corner to the men's section which was surprisingly in decent condition and browsed the left-over clothes at a pace that was perhaps a little too relaxed. After about fifteen minutes he had acquired one rucksack, socks, several pairs of boxer shorts, jeans, T-shirts and a hoodie. Managing to change into some clean clothes right then and there, topping off his new wardrobe with some decent looking knock-off Converse shoes. He even browsed the formal wear section and took a rather nice suit and tie for himself, just in case a "we survived the apocalypse party" was thrown in the near future.

It felt so good to be in clean, fresh clothes as just looking at his old ones crumpled on the floor made his stomach churn. To add insult several flies were now hovering over the clothes in a circular motion, indicating it was time to part ways with them. Out of his new possessions he liked his shoes the most by far. They may not have been practical and squeaked against the tiled floor, but there was no arguing with having a bit of style.

Ready and set to investigate Wilko he headed back towards the escalator, when suddenly from across the way a shimmer of light caught his attention. Heading over to investigate revealed a couple of dozen bottles of water just sitting there, in all their thirst-quenching glory. They wouldn't all squeeze into his new rucksack but that didn't stop him from trying. He just needed to leave room for pick 'n' mix sweets!

The rucksack was now heavier than he would have liked it to be, as was his bladder after downing two bottles of the clear stuff. But there would be plenty of time to rest once he got to Costco's, as he envisioned sprawling out on one of the king size display beds.

Turning to leave he was suddenly startled to the point of falling backwards into the metal shelving behind him. "Arrrgh!" He yelped as the shelves clattered to the floor into a twisted heap. It was then he looked up to see the silhouettes of two people stood before him. They seemed to be frozen to the spot, just staring down at him menacingly.

"Back up! I know how to use this" he said, whilst wildly swinging the metal railing. The two strangers loomed over him motionless, both stood in very peculiar, somewhat sexual positions. "Hello?" He said cautiously.

It quickly dawned on him that in his haste he had passed two mannequins, that someone had rather amusingly placed into compromising positions. So not only had he been very nearly scared to death, but now he was also slightly aroused to boot. It had been a few months after all.

Dusting himself off and taking a good look around to make sure no one had seen the embarrassing fall, he headed back down the escalator to Wilko as planned. All in all, despite the auspicious start to the day, things were starting to look up. New clothes, clean water and new material for the bank, not a bad result at all.

It was just a shame that the clattering of metal shelves had reached the rotting ears of two zombies who had finished dining upon their seagull lunch and were now heading in his direction. Proving that no matter the occasion there is always something just around the corner to spoil the fun.

Wilko was almost a total bust as the store had just about been picked clean as warned by a handwritten notice stuck to the shop entrance.

"Valued Customers."

"Due to the recent outbreak of stupidity and panic buying idiots, we are currently experiencing a shortage of, well everything."

"We expect supplies to be replenished once the zombies eat the people who decided that mountains of toilet paper were a better defence than actual weapons!"

"Thank you for your patience."

Whoever wrote the sign wasn't kidding, the shelves were bare, with the exception of three bags of compost and a variety of seeds. The compost would prove too much to carry and swing the metal pole at the same time if needed, but the seeds however would prove to be very helpful in the future. Potatoes, sweetcorn, tomatoes, cucumbers, strawberries and so much more were all quite easy to grow with a little know how. Even the sunflowers would prove to be useful for their oil and were good for the bees. Feeling very pleased with himself despite the lack of pick 'n' mix sweets, he left the store and headed back into the main square. It was here he was met by the sight of two very confused and partially feathered zombies.

Both wore black suits with three quarter length coats, one slim and tall, while the other was shorter and rounder than most. The rounder of the two sported a questionable moustache and wore a thin navy-blue tie while the taller of the two wore a rose-red bowtie. It wasn't clear, nor would it ever be to him what these two did for a living in a previous life. But it was there and then, these two were christened Zombie Stan and Zombie Ollie.

Zombie Stan and Zombie Ollie looked at the man before them with his nice clean clothes and knock-off Converse shoes, then back at one another displaying a look of disbelief. Had they been able to articulate the words they would have had some choice four letter expletives of their own. But a series of simple grunts would have to suffice.

They lunged with a coordinated attack but collided with each other instead, allowing their potential meal to make a hasty retreat. He headed in the direction of the multi-storey car park which was situated above the shopping centre before coming to an abrupt stop. The way was blocked by all manner of things, as it appeared that Costa coffee had caught fire at some point, bringing down the flats above, which brought the number of coffee shops in the town centre down to a mere five.

The corridor of shops was blocked by an impenetrable wall of rubble, twisted metal and rotten corpses dotted in between for good measure. Had there been more time he would have carefully scaled the wreckage, but the last thing he wanted, was to cut himself in doing so. A simple cut or scrape could be as fatal as a gunshot without the proper treatment in these undead times.

Zombie Stan was closing in with a ravenous look in his yellow eyes while Zombie Ollie had managed to trip over a bench, somehow wedging his arm between the slats. How these two had managed to trap a seagull was quite the mystery, but it would have been foolish to underestimate them. Doubling back on himself, running past the row of shops and scrambled over an overturned food van he managed to evade his attackers.

Glancing over his shoulder, he thought to himself "what sort of idiot would get stuck in a bench?" Before promptly managing to jam the metal bar between his legs, tripping and falling directly on to his face with a grotesque smack of skin meeting pavement. "What sort of idiot indeed."

He struggled back to his feet as stars blurred his vision, and searing pain shot down his legs. Zombie Stan and a now free Zombie Ollie were hot on his heels and quite literally spitting feathers from their snarling teeth. This was now a level playing field in terms of speed and endurance!

Limping onwards, doing his best to ignore the pain, his formally pristine knock-off Converse shoes were now badly scuffed up. He wanted to ditch the rucksack as it was weighing him down, but at the same time he could feel dehydration kicking back in despite his heavy bladder. As soon as he was free of these two, he would need a well-deserved drink of water.

Reaching the fountain once again, he leaned against the dirty black marble, keeping himself upright and caught his breath. Pushing onwards, past the stagnant, lime green waters as the undead alliance moved in, gaining ground all the while. He moved as quickly as his legs could carry him, heading towards the bus station. Most of the shops along the way were burnt out dead ends, forcing him onwards like a rat in a maze.

Reaching a bus stop, he took a moment to rest against the cold, mildewy plexiglass. It was here another decision had to be made.

Either stand his ground and fight, hoping for the best or head back, towards the safety of home, again hoping for the best.

Realising the metal railing was laying on the floor where he had fallen, the second option it had to be once more. Limping onwards towards the old post office, past the gym and the street food restaurant. With each step the deadly duo nipped literally at his heels as sadly, telling them to "sod off" repeatedly didn't seem to work.

The day had shown such promise but now it appeared that he was about to become the punchline in their stand-up routine. Almost out of urine fresh breath, his legs throbbing with shin splints, finally he reached the steps of somewhere that wasn't boarded up or burnt out, the Holiday Inn express hotel.

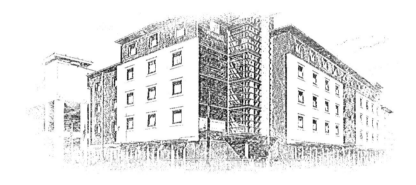

Zombie Stan and Zombie Ollie were right behind him which made it clear, either attempt to go inside now or become a very unhappy meal. Up the short flight of stairs and with a big push the double doors flew open, kicking up a cloud of dust that swirled directly up his nose and into his lungs. The dust made him cough and splutter, just like the mighty Dodge prior. He frantically felt around for the handles and slammed the doors behind him, applying the top and bottom deadlocks. Sealing Zombie Stan and Zombie Ollie outside with perplexed looks etched on their faces, like a pub had just shut without calling last orders.

This would have been an ideal time for a witty remark such as "Sorry gentleman, you don't appear to have a reservation." But all he could eek out between laboured breaths was "Shoes, ruined, idiots!"

It had all happened so quickly, that it dawned on him that no checks had been made to make sure the coast was clear. After all this was a hotel and held the potential to house several hundred zombies, all of whom would be a tad on the hungry side.

But rather surprisingly, apart from the occasional thud of bloated flesh against the main doors, it was silent, not a single stumbling corpse in sight. The main lobby, reception and bar were all within eyeshot and looked to be in top notch condition. He made certain the front door was properly secured and noticed a laminated sign stuck to the glass with thick, bold writing. He tore off the sticky-tape and turned the sign around, to better read it.

"To whom it may concern, it is with deep regret we must inform all of our customers and staff that this hotel will no longer be open for business until further notice."

"Once the pandemic comes to an end we will attempt to re-open in due course."

"Also please be advised that the continental breakfast does NOT include bacon!"

"Apologies for any inconvenience this may cause."

"The Manager."

The hotel was indeed empty, as it appeared in their haste the doors hadn't been locked. Only a fool or someone who was impressively brave would dare to enter, let alone dwell here. The hotel was situated in the heart of Stevenage, where a reward or two most likely awaited, but it also came with the most peril.

Zombie Stan and Zombie Ollie were only two of billion's more like them. The smell of fresh blood would carry across the wind, attracting whatever caught the sent. Only a few at first, but in time their numbers would grow, this was a certainty. But then he had a lightbulb moment.

"What if someone were to take a stand?" he thought. "What if this place were to become a haven in this desolate land and more to the point what could be gained from it?"

He walked around the lobby, tucking in a couple of chairs and ran his finger along the front desk, inspecting the thick layer of dust. He had always been the underling in his nine to five lifestyle, filled with deadlines and monthly performance reports. Just once he wanted to be on the other side and this place held the potential to offer him just that. Yes, this place would do nicely for his little brainwave project, after all the title of manager had quite a nice ring to it.

It may not have been as well stocked as Costco, but with a wide selection of beds and a potential kitchen full of canned goods, this place would do just fine for now.

Choosing to ignore Zombie Stan and Zombie Ollie who continually pounded on the front doors in vain, he took a deep breath of the stale air. Looking around he mentally mapped out the many tasks that lay ahead. Imagining a fortified hotel, bustling with people from all over the UK, who would trade all manner of things, just to stay one night. The world could be his for the taking, terms and conditions applying of course.

"Yes" he thought.

"The Manager will see you now."

Mr Kingsley

A small but vocal group had voiced their theories on how the outbreak started in an attempt to warn the world. Well, that and gain a million views on TikTok. But rather surprisingly, a handful of them were almost correct, minus the involvement of a certain Mr Gates, that was just ludicrous babble.

For a group of people whose main source of information had been social media newsfeeds, this was most impressive. Ruling out the involvement of disgruntled primates and underground lab monsters, the virus was indeed a man-made abomination, originating from a small laboratory. The word laboratory being applied very loosely as it was more of a fancy garden shed than anything else.

A university student by the name of Joseph Kingsley, had developed quite the dislike to mankind's dependence of modern technology and was determined to prove simpler methods were the way forward. One particular experiment of his involved trying to improve a carrier pigeons' performance. Mr Kingsley reasoned this was an attempt to prove these animals could be trusted with top secret messages for the armed forces, in a manner far superior to any electronic form of communication, after all you can't hack a pigeon.

However, it should be noted that this wasn't for any class project, Mr Kingsley simply had a lack of friends and an abundance of spare time. As a matter of fact, Mr Kingsley's idea of a good time was to take several shots of water every couple of hours to make sure he was healthy and hydrated. Not that there's anything wrong with that.

He travelled the length and breadth of the UK in pursuit of his craft even managing to spend some time in China, thanks to the bank of Mum and Dad. Unfortunately, he didn't really care for it there, as in his personal experience he found that the local children's behaviour was a bit too bratty for his liking.

Mr Kingsley once watched a child skipping down a road bouncing a little rubber ball on the ground repeatedly. Seemingly innocent but as the child came closer, he quickly realised that in fact that "ball" was actually a frog and the child was torturing it by slamming it on the ground. That evening he booked a return flight to England, deciding it best to continue his research there instead.

A mere month later he created a new type of bird feed, laced with performance enhancers, cognitive ability boosters and just a smidge of the avian flu to boost their immune systems. To say that Mr Kingsley was quite brilliant but also reckless when it came to his craft was somewhat of an understatement. The man didn't even wear gloves or a mask, which any self-respecting scientist will tell you is utter lunacy.

First to receive the super-feed was none other than a humble pigeon, which underneath their unappealing scruffy exterior are also brilliant creatures. Putting aside their unpopular social status as feathered beggars and ignoring the endless number of times they tend to pick up discarded cigarette ends mistaking them for food, they have some amazing abilities. Iron crystals in their beaks give these birds a sense of the Earth's magnetic field, acting as a tiny GPS unit.

Unfortunately for the humble pigeon, a misplaced Bunsen Burner led to a rather large explosion in Mr Kingsley's fancy garden shed, sending his project straight into the atmosphere. Once the unsuspecting avian species came into contact with the super-feed, it rapidly mutated into something else, jumping quickly from one species of bird to the next before anyone knew what was happening.

Once the virus had taken hold and quite literally taken flight, the unassuming birds contaminated all below their flight paths with disastrous results. In the weeks leading up to the cataclysmic events, it was noted on several news outlets that after some study, the common pigeon's equilibrium had suffered a dramatic change. In fact, this had caused them to do something very out of character for all pigeon kind, mass migrate.

In some circles this caused a small amount of unrest, but the rest of the world simply did not take this matter seriously enough. A major event like this should have captured the attention of the entire world, but typically this was overshadowed by perhaps an even bigger cock up, making the zombie outbreak pale in comparison. This of course being Brexit.

As for those brilliant Pigeons, well they hadn't quite got the hang of the migration thing. Many crashed landed into fresh water supplies, in turn speeding up the rate of infection. Others were sucked into various turbines along the way, the lucky ones however, landed in their new home of Antarctica. Where upon arrival they quickly froze to death and were eaten by sea lions, polar bears and the odd cannibalistic penguin. Perhaps they weren't so brilliant after all.

Lewis

Some people say they simply cannot believe the island of the United Kingdom has a bobsled team, but those people were mistaking it for the tiny island of Jamaica. Unfortunately, rather than being stuck on a zombie infested tropical paradise, Lewis and his two children had set up camp at a nature reserve called Mardley Heath.

It had been roughly two and a half years since a certain hotel began operating, not that Lewis knew anything about that. Lewis and his boys had moved to the countryside with nothing more than a three-man tent, a portable gas stove, sleeping bags and a few basic rations. But things were starting to look bleak for the trio, especially as they had run out of precious toilet paper. Getting his children to stay put for a considerable amount of time hadn't been the easiest of tasks as telling them they couldn't go out because of the virus somehow didn't sound scary enough.

Instead, Lewis had told his children "They had sworn an oath of solitude until pestilence had been purged from the land." Which sounded most valiant and heroic to the point people might have thought they carried a broadsword and went on quests. Of course, the reality was anything but.

Usually, they spent this time of year at one of the various Butlins holiday resorts, eating too much, frequenting the beach and generally having a good time. But good times were very much in short supply these days and their tent was a poor substitute for a holiday home.

Lewis was on his way back from a supply run which was always a risky business as he would have to leave his children behind to get around more quickly. But this particular run was fruitless, only finding a six pack of tinned dog food and some Turkish Delight, so nothing even remotely edible. The trip itself had been quite uneventful, as there weren't any signs of life in the surrounding area besides the occasional rabbit or rat. Lewis had tried to sneak up on the rabbits where possible, but they were always too fast for him, so he mastered the art of the snare trap.

Feeling defeated and concerned for his children's welfare, Lewis returned to the campsite only to be confronted by a gathering of zombies trying to get inside their tent. In total there were five of the beasts, all working in unison to get the gooey human treats inside. These ones were in an advanced state of decay, their clothes blackened and in tatters, only held together by a stitching of foul-smelling pus. They were badly balding, their skin a horrid greyish green with huge yellow blisters over their arms and hands.

Horrified, Lewis instinctively took aim and prepared to throw the tins of dog food directly at their heads. Five zombies, six tins of food, meant he would have to be precise to inflict an effective blow each time.

Poised and with concentrated aim Lewis threw the first tin which sailed gracefully through the air, well as gracefully as a dog food projectile possibly could. But missed every single one of the zombies by a clear foot, ricocheting off the nylon tent and hitting one square in the nether regions. Lewis had never seen a zombie wince in pain and crumple to the ground until that moment, but it seemed to be rather effective and now there were only four to deal with. Once again in unison the remaining foes turned towards Lewis and lined up, seeming to protect themselves from the same fate. At first glance you would have been forgiven for thinking they were a tattered five aside football team, protecting their side from conceding a goal.

Again, Lewis took aim, took a run up and with everything he had, launched missile number two. This one hit the zombie on the far-left square between the eyes with a squelchy thwack. However, it did not have the desired effect, only serving to enrage the zombie, rallying the others into action. Then suddenly something grabbed Lewis's waist from behind, instinctively he lashed out and bashed his attacker with a stiff shot of pedigree chums finest. Only to realise he had in fact struck his son Martin square in the face!

Martin was only eight years old and was a bit of a wimp at the best of times, let alone almost being knocked out by his own dad. His other son Tom who was eleven stood directly behind, watching everything unfold. Had she been around Tom's first instincts would have been to WhatsApp his mum and tell her what had happened.

"Dad just hit Martin with a tin of dog food, can you come and get us, also can you bring my phone charger."

Lewis had never really had a good relationship with the boy's mum, so the end of the world was actually a nice break from her. But still, even with her long gone her voice echoed in his ears. "Well done Lewis, dad of the year yet again!"

But there was no time to get hung up on the past, not with four zombies advancing on them. The undead awkwardly shuffled over their comrade, who laid on the ground, clutching its gentleman's area and wailing horribly. Had its intentions not been on the munchie side Lewis could have almost felt sorry for it. Martin stood there stunned, not sure whether to cry or run away, so Lewis quickly made the decision for him.

"Catch" Lewis said to Tom tossing the remaining tins of dog food. Tom wasn't usually the most coordinated of children but to his dad's surprise caught the tins out of the air with ease. Hoisting Martin over his shoulder Lewis commanded Tom.

"Follow me now, quickly!" which he did not need telling twice.

The trio made their way across a beaten path, it had been raining consistently over the past few days which made the way extra slick with thick mud and ash. The skies had been darker than ever lately, with ash raining down from the heavens. Lewis watched this change of weather with great interest, usually where there is smoke, there's fire. But as far as he could tell, nothing in the immediate area was burning, still thick black and grey ash continued to fall daily, covering the world around them. It turns out, when mixed, mud, ash and copious amounts of rain, make a gloopy clay like substance. Which made walking perilous enough let alone sprinting at full speed with a child over one shoulder.

They frantically passed through scratching bramble vines, careful to avoid rabbit holes and snare traps that littered the way, rapidly reaching a waist high fence. The fence was old and held together with thick, rusted bolts, surrounded by giant hogweeds. They were careful not to touch the sap as it contains toxins, activated by natural light that can cause nasty skin lesions and burns.

Just beyond the fence was a secluded country lane where they would be able to rest for a moment and catch their collective breath. Tom went to place his hands onto the fence before Lewis quickly grabbed him by the sleeve, as barbed wire ran the entire length. Judging by the clumps of greyish green flesh, this was how the zombie five aside team had gained access to the field. Catching themselves on the giant hogweeds, explaining the disgusting blisters all over their extremities.

"Careful yeah? We don't have any antibiotics left" said Lewis as a wide-eyed Tom nodded his head in agreement.

Lewis put Martin down and removed his coat, placing it across the barbed wire "come on mate, over you go" he said to Tom who did as he was asked. "Okay it's your turn now" Lewis said to Martin who had been silently crying the entire time. He gave a brave little nod and hoisted himself over, as Tom helped his brother onto the other side.

The gathering shambled ever closer towards the trio, until they fell afoul of the rabbit hole minefield, buying them some precious time. Lewis joined the boys on the other side of the fence and turned to Martin, giving him a big hug.

"You alright mate?" he asked, but it was clear his face was going to badly bruise. "I'm so sorry! I thought you were one of them." Martin was holding his cheek tightly, as if he were to let go his head might fall off altogether.

Branches twisted and cracked with the approaching sound of the dead, indicating it was time to make haste. In an ideal world they would have laid low for a while and headed back once it was safe to do so. Well, in an actual ideal world people wouldn't come back from the dead with a severe case of the munchies, but as they used to say on Love Island "it is what it is."

But Lewis knew there was no going back, even just to collect their things. As once a zombie had caught the scent of fresh meat, the area was tainted for the foreseeable future. Zombies are nothing if not persistent when it comes to a good meal. There are around sixty-thousand miles of blood vessels in the human body which if laid from end to end would stretch around the world more than twice. It was these, that zombies craved, able to sniff out fresh blood like decaying bloodhounds. Of course, there are certain ways and means to mask one's scent, but none of them are all that pleasant.

The trio stood at the edge of the country lane as the dead inched in closer all the while. Cold and wet, they had to quickly choose between two possible routes. Right would take them deeper into the countryside, which may have been the safer option but also offered little in the way of shelter with even less promise of food and water.

Left would lead though a small village called Knebworth and then into the town of Stevenage which while shelter was a guarantee, it also came with the heightened risk of running into even larger gatherings. It was somewhere around midday, the sun already starting to disappear beyond the horizon. Meaning to quote a formally popular fantasy saga, winter was coming.

With this in mind, left it had to be, much to the dismay of five hungry zombies. Along the way Tom had taken it upon himself to try and raise Martin's sprits by presenting him with a formidable looking stick to defend himself with, whilst keeping a slightly better stick for himself. ,

"En-garde!" Tom called out, taking what he thought to be a classic fencing position. Martin reluctantly held his cheek and frowned. "En-garde!" Tom called out again as Martin eventually cracked a smile and also took what he imagined to be a classic fencing pose. Tom was pretty good when it came to looking after his little brother, feeling it his duty after being through quite a harrowing experience himself just prior to Black Sunday.

At seven years old Tom realised that he could sneak downstairs after everyone else had gone to sleep for the evening, that way he could eat anything from the fridge that he wanted without ever being caught. Leftover roast chicken mixed with chocolate spread in a sandwich, the last quarter of birthday cake to himself, it was all up for grabs.

Creeping down was always the hardest part though, having to navigate the house in total darkness like a tiny ninja, but he soon became a master of his craft. One evening they had ordered pizza which beckoned to him in the middle of the night as once again Tom crept through the darkness. Getting down the stairs was always the worst part, desperately trying to avoid the fabled squeaky step, but once clear of this, Tom could let down his guard. He crept through the living room and into the kitchen when he suddenly heard the distinctive sound of cutlery clink on the countertop.

Bathed in the glow of the microwave clock light, Tom saw the outline of a skinny man, sloppily eating the contents of the fridge. Luckily, the man didn't see or hear Tom, but Tom saw him alright. The skinny man's lips smacked together as food fell from his disgusting mouth, all washed down with milk straight from the carton. Tom had been terrified and rightfully so, as he slowly backed away and went upstairs to alert his dad. But Lewis made far too much noise getting up to investigate, by the time he got downstairs the culprit was nowhere to be seen.

Lewis put it down to a combination of too many scary stories and a child's active imagination, but it was enough to put Tom off milk for a good while. This may have happened before the events of Black Sunday, but Tom couldn't help feeling like that was his very first encounter with a zombie, perhaps even patient zero for all he knew.

From that day onwards Lewis started to spend as much time with his boys as possible, keen to reassure them everything was okay. One of their favourite activities had been walking their little dog in the local woodlands, not too dissimilar from where they had been camping. Lewis had let his boy's name the dog which turned out to be quite the mistake as they settled on calling him Onions. This was solely done to make fun of their dad who suffered from Alliumphobia, the fear of onions and garlic.

Unfortunately, and very much unbeknownst to the boys their little dog had long since become a meal for them. Onions had simply been too yappy for his own good and lacked the basic instincts to make it out in the world alone. By keeping him, they were condemning themselves to certain death, so it was a necessary sacrifice, just not an easy one to make. That day, chopping Onions really did bring tears to Lewis's eyes.

It was just as well, as one of the governments final laws was that all pets, no matter how small had to be destroyed. As the virus could be carried over to man's best friend acting as a "reservoir" to be reintroduced to humans at a later date. These were quite literally reservoir dogs. Luckily, Onions was one of the uninfected, which was just as well, seeing the trio had eaten him.

As they pushed on through the winding country lanes, they passed a couple of pubs along the way. The Red Lion and the North Star, both of which had all the windows and doors boarded up with impenetrable solid steel security screens. As Lewis didn't happen to have a spare crowbar in his back pocket they kept moving onwards. There was a certain smell that hung in the air, the almost tangible scent before a storm. It was fresh and invigorating, serving to raise their morale, but after being stuck in a field all that time, just about anything was a much-needed morale boost.

Along the way, Tom and Martin marvelled at the most basic of things, squealing with excitement when they happened across an old-style red phone box. Lewis explained that people used to put money in the slot and dial numbers, which would allow you to speak to anyone in the world. Even if back in Lewis's day he mainly used them to ask his mum for a lift home after a long night out on the town. It made Lewis sad to know his boys would never know the true joys of childhood, but that was just the way things were now.

The trio walked for what seemed like hours as Lewis made sure to keep an eye on the skies for any infected birds, thankfully this deep into the apocalypse, they seemed to be few and far between as their wings rotted away. The effects of the invigorating air began to wear off as the trio began to feel tired and achy by the time they finally reached the outskirts of Stevenage. The roads were sticky from the ash and rain combination, pulling at their shoes with every step like Velcro. Tom managed to slip out of his shoe's multiple times, leading to very damp socks, even so he remained in good spirits.

After walking up what seemed to be the steepest road in all of England, they happened across a large road sign that had been repainted with some bizarre information. Before the events of Black Sunday anyone caught defacing such a sign would have been issued a fine ranging from £50 to £200 but on this occasion, this would prove to be just the lifeline the Trio needed.

"Welcome to Stevenage, Home to the best hotel this side of the apocalypse, the Holiday Inn Express, ask for The Manager."

Lewis knew of this hotel having been in the area on several occasions. Of course, he was reluctant to get his hopes up, but there was a certain appeal in taking the chance. To make a sign so bold like this implied safety in numbers, food and water, even if he was getting a little ahead of himself. But his optimism was contagious, lifting the boys spirits even further, beyond that of formidable looking sticks.

They could have taken their chances by themselves, moving from house to house, gathering what they could until something more suitable came along. Perhaps moving out to another secluded spot in the countryside. But Lewis had to think of his boys, plus the thought of clean blankets and soft beds pretty much sealed the deal. In hindsight perhaps he should have put more thought into this decision, but three hungry tummies would be enough to cloud anyone's judgement.

"Fancy staying in a hotel tonight boys?" he asked.

The two grinned from ear to ear, until Martin remembered just how much his face hurt, instead opting to give a meek thumbs up. It would be at least another hour of walking at best, plus extra time for tired little legs but they needed to make haste if they were to arrive before nightfall. Heading in the most direct route possible, the streets were eerily quiet, with every house looking like something out of a horror movie. Many doors and windows had been left wide open and the ones that were shut had terrible bloody smears all over. The hotel was starting to look more and more like their only salvation.

Still with a considerable distance to go, they stopped at a little corner shop that had its shutter halfway down, or up depending on the outlook. Here they managed to gather some provisions which included chocolate for the boys. They stuffed their pockets with Snickers and Maltesers, opting to replace the gaps on the shelves with Turkish Delight for someone who would appreciate the unique taste. It is simply amazing what a bit, or in this case ninety-four grams of sugar per person can do, even if it was all terribly out of date.

Now all three of them had boundless energy and were covering ground fast, at this rate they would arrive at the hotel well ahead of schedule. Moving through the evac zones, so far not seeing anything of concern. Lewis even began to wonder if they had spent too much time out in the countryside, perhaps the worst had blown over and everybody else was having a great time at Butlins Bognor Regis.

Occasionally there would be a rustle of a plastic bag or the clank of a metal gate slamming shut with the wind, causing the trio to jump out of their skin and quicken the pace. Along the way Lewis picked up an old piece of fence with two long protruding nails as a form of self-defence. Tom was quick to dub this simple weapon as the "thagomizer" named after the spikes on the end of a Stegosaurus' tail.

Back in their tent dwelling days Lewis's weapon of choice had been a trusty cricket bat, just like Shaun of the dead. But Lewis had hit his last innings a couple of weeks back when he swung for a particularly aggressive house cat, hitting the corner of a wall instead, breaking his beloved bat clean in two. His new weapon was basic but would prove effective should the situation arise.

Then, like a beacon in the oasis that was the zombie desert, there stood a large white van that looked to be in somewhat decent condition. This was most unusual as cars were a rare commodity as most vehicles had rusted away, unloved and unused. This particular van had been previously used to transport organic produce to customers far and wide. As Lewis moved in for a closer inspection, he chuckled to himself as he read aloud an amusing warning to any would be fruit thieves that had been etched onto the back doors. "No pineapples are left in this vehicle overnight."

Lewis gripped the matt black door handle and pulled it open as the lock made a satisfying popping sound. Any sense of optimism was soon dashed though, as the smell of a thousand rotting fruit and vegetables surrounded them, bringing tears to their eyes.

Without the need for words, the trio agreed this was not the vehicle of choice for them after all, but then Tom spotted something far more promising at the end of the street. A rather sporty looking car, big and brash with faded racing stripes. In this case it appeared that lightning did indeed strike twice as this vehicle looked to have fared even better than the van.

"Dad what about that one?" asked Tom, as Lewis wiped away the tears from his eyes and cautiously moved towards the car. Upon further inspection they were ecstatic to see a set of keys left inside, dangling from the oddly placed ignition switch. Whoever left this car behind must have done in a hurry they thought as it was quite the rarity to find keys anywhere close to the vehicle itself. These days keys were usually snugly tucked in the pockets of the dead as they wandered around aimlessly miles away from where they belonged.

The paint had been a deep shade of blue but now severely weather worn, almost like someone had randomly painted little white clouds over the bodywork. This coupled with a lovely shade of moss green created a canvas that Mr Bob Ross would have been proud of. The tyres were a little flat, but for the most part still looked drivable despite the toll mother nature had inflicted upon them.

Lewis took a quick look in the back seat to ensure nothing sinister lurked there, then pulled at the front door handle. It opened with a less satisfying groan, as the two boys squealed with joy, once again getting a little ahead of themselves. The car was a bit audacious for Lewis's taste, but after remaining silent and hidden away for the past couple of years, perhaps loud and audacious is just what the doctor ordered he thought.

Lewis took a cautious look around and skyward, making sure they were indeed alone and leaned in to clutch the keys. The ignition switch was on the left-hand side but still worked all the same once turned. The car spluttered and tried to turn over but failed as it quickly became apparent there wasn't any petrol left in the tank. Lewis couldn't help but wonder who would leave a perfectly good car just because it ran out of petrol. But then again perhaps the owner had been getting petrol when the worst happened, he assumed.

Lewis walked around the car giving it a thorough look over, noting all the marks and topping it off with a couple of traditional kicks to the wheels. "Hmm, I don't know much about this make of car, logo says it's a Dodge. But if it goes forward then it can't be all that bad, I suppose. You two climb in the back, I'm just gonna pop over there for a minute, okay?" Lewis instructed the boys, whilst pointing towards another rusted out car sat in a driveway just opposite.

Martin and Tom ditched their formidable sticks, climbed into the back and closed the doors. Despite their dad leaving them, they felt a lot safer within the confines of the car. The seat leather was cold to touch and well-worn and cracked in places, exposing dirty looking yellow cushioning underneath. But it was still far more comfortable than sitting on a damp sleeping bag.

Once settled the boys could see their dad rummaging through the overgrown gardens, clearly, he was on the hunt for something. For a moment Lewis disappeared out of sight behind a tall hedge which made them a bit apprehensive, but soon reappeared on the other side. Now with a green garden hose and a red plastic recycling bin that had seen better days as he walked past them and back towards the rancid white van.

41

Tom and Martin struggled to see what their dad was up to, but it appeared he was sticking the end of the hosepipe into the van's petrol tank, which in this case was not a euphemism. Tom roughly knew what was happening as he cast his mind back to an old episode of the Simpsons where the character Ottoman had done the same thing.

Lewis took a deep breath and began to suck on the other end of the hosepipe, which did not look at all pleasant. He gagged and retched, spitting out clumps of thick black and green sludge. It took a fair amount of perseverance, but finally precious petrol began to flow into a recycling bin that Lewis had placed at the ready. It took several nauseating minutes but soon he had collected a decent amount of fuel as he brought the sloshy contents over and angled it into the Dodge's petrol tank.

Looking in through the back window, Lewis gave the boys a reassuring thumbs up as they sat back in preparation for their journey. Martin, who was still very sore but putting on a brave face gave Tom a nudge and handed him something. It was a phone just like the one Tom used to have. Tom smiled and pushed the power button, but nothing happened "It's dead" he said disappointedly.

Martin gave him another nudge, directing his brother's attention to the footwell, where there lay a USB charger. The boys looked at each other and smiled, chocolate and a phone, this day wasn't turning out so bad after all. Now with some fuel in the tank, Lewis climbed into the driver's seat and mentally mapped out the best route to take on foot as a backup plan.

"Fingers crossed boys" he said.

The car groaned like a teenager who had been rudely awoken, asking for five more minutes. Lewis gave it a second and tried again, the audacious car tried its best to come back to life but still nothing. The boys let out a collective sigh.

"Come on you two, fingers crossed like I asked yeah? We need all the luck we can get." Lewis closed his eyes and placed his head on the steering wheel, as he muttered something not meant for young ears. He turned the key and pushed down on the accelerator, willing it back into existence. The boys crossed their fingers as asked. The old Dodge let out a cough, then a clunk, then finally a ferocious roar! The trio cheered and whooped as excitement filled their souls for the first time in a long time. The dashboard lit up with all manner of colourful lights, flashing and beeping away at them. From check engine to low tire pressure, it was a digital rainbow of warning signs.

Lewis noticed that the odometer happened to read "eighty-eight-thousand, eight-hundred and eighty-eight miles" exactly. Once upon a time he had taken a few tarot reading classes to impress an old girlfriend. He recalled the number eight was somewhat of a lucky number, as it was meant to help you make decisions, to move forward in life, in this case quite literally it seemed.

"Who would leave a car liked this behind?" Lewis said aloud as he patted the steering wheel as if telling the car well done. He looked over his shoulder towards the boys and was greeted with an outstretched hand, holding a phone and wire.

"We found these; do you think you could charge it please?" Tom asked.

Lewis took the phone and charger, plugging one end into a modified cigarette lighter. In the passenger footwell was a phone holder that had lost its suction. With a little spit, Lewis applied the suction cup to the windscreen and waited a moment for the phone to turn on. The phone flickered with a reassuring battery charging symbol, then fully came back to life with a home screen. It quickly became apparent this had been a work phone of some sort and didn't require a PIN code to gain access. The notifications went wild, pinging over and over as a back log of messages that made it through before the network shut down demanded to be heard. There was a notable text message from someone called Paul, reading; "why aren't you at work? It's not the end of the world you know!"

It had been so long since the boys were excited about anything, but today was like hitting the jackpot as for a short while, Lewis felt like they had a semblance of childhood back.

"Let's turn the phone off for now, make sure it has a good charge before we get to the hotel, yeah? After all, I'm sure you two have missed taking selfies!"

They both nodded, resisting every fibre of their being to take hold of the phone until the screen went dark again. Lewis closed the driver's side door and once they all had their seatbelts on, they set off through the evac zones. The tyres made an awful drumming sound as they slowly drove along, ensuring the phone slurped up as much second-hand electricity as possible. The car defied all logic, there was no way it should be moving forward and yet here they were, cruising along to spend a night at a hotel.

"You know, a lucky car such as this deserves a name, what do you two think?" asked Lewis.

Martin and Tom quietly conferred with each other for a minute, before proudly announcing that the car should be called "Dreadnought."

"That's an interesting name, I mean I was thinking more along the lines of Lola or something, but Dreadnought does sound cool," said Lewis. "What made you think of that?"

The name dreadnought had been stuck in Tom's head for a while, as it was one of the last things he had learnt about in school, back when school was the norm. "Dreadnought was a type of battleship used in World War One, it was one of the largest and most powerful of its kind!" Explained Tom.

Lewis looked in the rear-view mirror to gauge Martin's reaction, who nodded in agreement. "Dreadnought huh? that's a tough name for a tough old car, I like it!"

The boys sat back pleased with themselves, they had never named a car before, let alone a lucky one.

Dreadnought was large and difficult to manoeuvre through the overgrown streets, no thanks to a lack of power-steering fluid. But as the car crept forward, gradually gaining speed, it began to cooperate with Lewis at the helm. The roar of the engine combined with the high-pitched whine of the breaks attracted the attention of quite a few zombies. The majority of whom were trapped in their former homes, now all riled up as meals on wheels drove past.

After fifteen minutes of driving, darkness crept in, indicating it was time to get a move on as Lewis put the accelerator down as much as he dared. They passed several retail parks, all of which were littered with the undead, luckily these zombies lacked the ability to keep up with the noisy car. Soon they passed one of Stevenage's well-known landmarks, Six Hills Way, which had previously been debated for decades if it was a rare historical monument or actually the handiwork of the Devil.

The story went that the Devil himself sat overlooking the Great North Road being constructed and was in such a temper that he heaved up six great clods of earth and threw them at travellers. Although the reality was that Roman-British aristocrats were laid to rest there. Their bones long decaying underneath the earth, which meant it was a safe bet they wouldn't be coming back from the dead anytime soon. Which was just as well, as modern-day zombies were bad enough to deal with let alone armour plated and sword wielding ones.

A gathering shuffled in between the mounds of earth, lured towards the sound of the passing car engine. They were all so brittle looking, as if a stiff breeze would cut them down with ease. Whilst a couple were spritelier than the rest, they were clearly no danger for the trio.

Upon reaching a roundabout, there was yet another custom sign, only this one appeared to be moving. Not much but just enough to make Lewis slowdown in order to read it. Upon closer inspection it was clear someone had fixed a board to a zombie, who in turn was chained to a railing. Had Lewis not previously struck another unfortunate zombie in the goolies earlier then perhaps this would have been the strangest sighting today. But as it stood, this only ranked at number two on the weird-o-meter for the day.

He slowed to a stop, the car breaks letting out a noise like a cat whose tail had been stood on. The trio read the sign aloud together, like an apocalyptic karaoke session, "The Holiday Inn Express, haven for all, right at the next roundabout, ask for The Manager."

If that weren't odd enough, Lewis could have sworn the zombie waved as they drove past, but the zombie had been pinned into that position thanks to his mysterious captor, simply known as "The Manager." Shrugging it off they continued until they finally reached the next roundabout, turning right as prompted.

The ash was even worse here, almost three times thicker compared to the countryside, hanging in the air, choking the life out of everything it touched. Dreadnought, whilst old and battle scarred glided along the roads, as if floating on blackened clouds.

Finally, as promised, the Holiday Inn Express appeared before them. Not to be confused with a similar looking hotel just across the street. Unbeknownst to Lewis the other hotel had been taken over by a gathering of formidable and particularly aggressive zombies.

But Lewis had a keen sense of direction and managed to follow the correct signs. On arrival it was clear that somebody had put a lot of work into this place. All the front windows had been blacked out and barbed wire ran along the perimeter. This was broken up by the occasional set of vital organs hanging from them, which actually added a nice splash of colour against an otherwise dreary concrete grey backdrop. In the middle, just over the main entrance was another sign that simply read, "Welcome."

Besides the welcome sign, there weren't any other signs of life, at least not from the car window. The boys peered towards the ominous looking hotel and back towards their dad.

"Do you think it's safe?" asked Tom nervously.

"Only one way to find out, otherwise we are all sleeping in Dreadnought tonight."

At first glance anyone would have thought it was a gritty, horrid little stop in the middle of the apocalypse. One that probably did not have a happy ending for those that chose to check in. Sometimes things really are only surface deep, but with fingers still crossed, the trio hoped the inside would be very different. Perhaps it would prove to be a paradise of clean sheets and room temperature water at the very least.

Lewis parked the car across the street in the Matalan car park, which under normal circumstances only allowed a two-hour stay, providing you had paid and displayed. But these weren't exactly normal circumstances, despite this, Lewis had a little nagging voice. One that told him to move the car a bit later, just in case, as knowing his luck, a stray traffic warden was probably lurking just around the corner keen to pounce.

The town centre itself seemed to be clear of any gatherings and the ledges of the surrounding buildings appeared to be bird free, which only served to make the trio even more nervous. Usually this was a bustling town centre, filled with people doing their weekly shop. The town had once offered everything a growing boy needed from McDonalds to Weatherspoon's, but personally, Lewis had never been that keen on the whole "let's go downtown" thing. Instead opting to order online where he could.

He treated people like zombies long before they actually were, often crossing the road or pretending to be on the phone to bypass any undesirables. For fear they may infect him with their insanity or the worst-case scenario, ask if he was happy with his energy supplier, full disclosure, he wasn't. But today Lewis needed to be braver than he had ever known as he ushered the boys from the car.

"Don't forget the phone dad" Martin said through a muffled voice.

Clearly his priorities were a bit lacking, but anything that took his mind off his now swollen face were very much welcome. Lewis tried to hide his own concern, but Tom hadn't quite yet mastered the art of little white lies as he looked at his brother with a mixture of disgust and horror. Lewis quickly moved them along before he could say anything upsetting. With only a partially charged phone and car keys in their possession, they walked over to the main entrance. Lewis thought about bringing the thagomizer with them, but first impressions still counted for something in this world and he didn't want to look aggressive in his approach.

There were makeshift bollards dotted around, comprised of rubbish bins filled with sand and wrapped in even more barbed wire. They were spread out unevenly making it easy for any lumbering zombies to get snagged on which must have worked a treat judging by the tangled, bloody strips of clothing swaying gently in the breeze.

"Yellow" mumbled Martin as Lewis looked at him oddly.

"Sorry, what was that?" he asked.

"Yellow, look yellow ducks" said Martin as he pointed with his one free hand.

He was right, along the entrance and in the raised flower beds were hundreds of yellow plastic bath ducks. Some were plain old ducks; some wore sunglasses while others wore rainbow wigs. In that moment they were surrounded by a gathering of hundreds of little yellow ducks. It was all a bit strange, but at the same time, rather amusing, adding a welcoming feeling to the place. Tom leant down and grabbed two of them, handing one to Martin, again secretly making sure to keep the best one for himself.

"Thank you" said Martin as he studied the plastic bath accessory. "Look it's wearing little sunglasses."

The boys both laughed and placed a duck each in their pockets, then turned their attention back to their dad. Lewis inspected the wide and tall doors, trying in vain to peer through the blackened glass. He pushed and pulled on the handles, but someone had reinforced them from within. Stuck to the frame was an A4 plastic pouch with a neatly folded piece of paper inside, which Lewis removed to find a set of instructions and began to read aloud.

"Welcome to the Holiday Inn Express, we are so glad you made it."

"Please ring the bell three times and state your intentions through the letter box."

"The Manager will be right with you."

Lewis neatly folded the letter, placing it back in the pouch and looked around the frame for a bell. Hanging to one side was a thick brown rope, similar to which school children used to climb in PE. Attached to the end was a large brass bell, which appeared to be loud enough to wake the dead, in this case quite literally. There was a moment of apprehension amongst the trio as Lewis took hold of the rope. Martin who was still clutching his face with one hand, used his free one to tug at his dad's shirt.

"Too loud, they will hear us" his voice still partially muffled as Tom nodded in agreement.

"No one answers and we run back to Dreadnought and get the hell out of here okay?" Lewis said reassuringly as possible.

Although the high pitch of his voice betrayed his true feelings.

The boys had little choice but to agree with their dad despite sharing the same feeling of dread about the whole situation. Lewis rang the bell once, twice, three times, as instructed with each clang louder than the previous.

"Erm, hello, three humans here, anyone home?" Lewis called out, as he crouched down to speak through the letter box. "We followed the signs; we are unarmed and would like to stay please."

They waited for what seemed like forever, but the door didn't budge, there were no sounds of movement from the other side. Besides the collective sound of their heartbeats pounding in unison, the only sounds of movement were that of sudden growls in the distance. The dead had indeed woken.

Lewis had to physically hold the back of the boy's coats to stop them from bolting, as he was keen to give this Manager character a chance to open up. But the growls grew ever closer, like a literal dinner bell had been rung, beckoning the hungry beasts.

"Dad let's just go, please!" pleaded Tom as he and Martin moved from side to side on their tippy toes nervously, as if walking on hot coals.

But it was too late, a gathering of around seventy zombies emerged in the distance and were moving with an urgent pace. They quickly passed through the bus station and would arrive at the hotel shortly as Lewis grabbed the rope and rang the bell again, once, twice, three times.

This only seemed to enrage the gathering as they focused all their attention on the trio. The undead drew ever closer as the yellows of their eyes and blackened, snarling teeth became visible. The front runners couldn't have turned all that long ago, still looking vaguely human, except for the odd missing limb. While the ones at the back were more contorted, like circus acts gone wrong, dragging their twisted and mangled frames as fast as they could manage.

They carried with them a great stink that was almost debilitating even at a distance, so bad was it that plants seemed to wilt as the dead stampeded through the town. The gathering spilled onto the street like a rogue wave crashing onto a beach, kicking up a great, suffocating ash cloud in their wake.

They growled and roared with a fiendish frenzy as they closed in on their prey, quickly cutting the trio off from Dreadnought. Lewis readied to pull the boys out of harm's way when he felt something pull him sharply backwards. Still clutching the back of the boy's coats, they in turn were also yanked backwards, crossing the now open threshold as suddenly the doors slammed shut in front of them. Tom and Martin stumbled, losing their footing, knocking their dad over. Lewis groaned as he took a nasty spill to the cold, hard floor, but still had the sense to cushion the boy's fall. One of the plastic ducks let out a high-pitched squeak under their weight, announcing their arrival like clown's comedy prat-falling from a car.

They lay in a huddled mess trying to gather their bearings when the distinctive sound of metal clanking filled their senses. Deadbolts were being applied and a metal bar clumsily dragged into place. This was promptly followed by the sounds of rotting flesh slamming against the entrance doors. The frame bent inwards, under the sheer mass of the gathering, straining to stay intact. The trio sprung back to their feet and huddled together, their heads on a swivel, taking in their new surroundings. They were in a large reception area, which had to be the cleanest place this side of the apocalypse. They were suddenly surrounded by clean white tables, all with chairs neatly tucked in. Each table topped with napkins, glasses, cutlery, complete with a lit candle, all placed with great care and precision.

On the opposite side was a long white desk that ran for half the length of the room, with a single black book placed directly in the middle.

Lewis was still trying to collect himself when he finally saw their saviour, a tall, thin man with his back turned towards them. It was hard to tell in the dim candlelight, but he appeared to be dressed in a clean black suit, trying to reach some sort of apparatus.

"Do take a seat, I will be right with you" said the man politely whilst keeping his back to the trio.

Lewis didn't need telling twice and with a single look instructed the boys to comply as they quickly sat on a bright orange sofa, tucked into the corner. They sat down in silence, observing the tall man pulling and pushing a variety of locks, securing the hotel from any undead invaders. Oddly, amongst all of the commotion, Lewis couldn't help but notice the man's footwear seemed out of place in comparison to his nice clean suit. These being a pair of well worn, black and white, knock-off Converse shoes.

The man began to pull on a second rope that threaded through the wall, this one suspended high off the ground, leading around the corner towards the local library. At the end of which was an identical brass bell that began to loudly ring out. Clearly the tall man was well prepared, which came as a massive reassurance to the new arrivals. The gooey thumps of zombie meat against the thick wooden doors slowed, as most of the gathering broke away, moving towards the secondary bell, like well trained dogs.

Some stragglers could not be deterred however as they had the scent of fresh blood in their rotting nasal cavities. The tall man ceased ringing the second bell and tied off the rope to a hook halfway up the wall.

"Sorry about this, gatherings can be such a nuisance, can't they?" he said whilst fussing with yet another rope.

The tall man uncoiled a third rope that also led to the outside, although there was no bell at the end of this one. Instead, this one lowered a bucket of putrid red contents through a makeshift serving hatch to the ground outside. It was almost as if Kevin McAllister had designed this peculiar place, Lewis half expected the zombies to get thwacked by paint cans at any given moment. Whatever the contents of the bucket were, they seemed to appease the remaining zombies as the dull roar of the gathering subsided and were replaced with content, sloppy chomps.

The tall man brushed himself down and turned with arms wide open. "Welcome one and all to the Holiday Inn Express, Stevenage, pleased to make your acquaintances, I am The Manager."

Lewis stood up and whispered to the boys to stay put, while The Manager quickly took his place behind the reception desk and waited for his new guest to approach.

"Thank you, I'm Lewis and these are my two boys, Martin and Tom." The boys gave a meek wave and continued sitting in silence, taking in their new surroundings.

"It's very nice to meet you all, so, tell me, how long will you be staying with us?" The Manager asked, getting directly to the point of the matter.

"Um, I don't know, I guess as long as possible please?"

The Manager grinned from ear to ear. "Well, the hotel offers one-hundred and twenty-nine stylish bedrooms at affordable prices and has a welcoming lounge and bar that's great for relaxing in."

His manner was one of confidence, like he really knew what he was talking about. If the reception area were anything to go by then the rest of the hotel would do quite nicely. Lewis was keen to play it cool despite the close call with the gathering as he really needed a win.

Plus, quite frankly sleeping in the same car as two flatulent boys was not on the agenda for the evening. But what did The Manager mean by "affordable" exactly? Lewis wondered.

Money had long since gone the way of the dodo, in fact Lewis had used the last of his notes to start a campfire long ago. Which under the currency and bank notes act of 1928 was a criminal offence, but given the circumstances it was probably acceptable in the eyes of the law.

Lewis hadn't encountered many other people in his travels over the past couple of years, but the few he had met were always willing to trade the odd few bits. Admittedly they would usually try to rob him immediately afterwards, but Lewis always flew into defence mode which mostly consisted of yelling and running away. In any case the only two items in his possession, the car keys and phone were simply too valuable to trade for board. At least until they knew if this place was the real deal or not.

"I'm sorry, but I don't have much in the way of payment, all I can offer you is my sincere thanks for now."

The Manager looked somewhat befuddled, like Lewis had skipped reading the full terms and conditions, clicking on agree regardless.

"Ah well in that case I can set you all up with our super saver package if that suits yourselves?"

Lewis looked back at his boys to gauge their reactions, but they were no longer paying attention to the conversation. Instead, they were up off the sofa, each picking up a spoon and whispering "En-garde" again accompanied with what they considered to be classic fencing poses.

It was good to see them happy, there had been short supply of enjoyment in recent months. A tent in the British countryside whilst nice in the summer, wasn't the ideal place to raise two boys. Combine that with a literal dog's dinner and you have the makings of some very depressing times.

"Listen, I will do whatever it takes, help out around here, do supply runs, anything okay? Please just let us stay, just don't send us back out there" Lewis whispered, not wanting the boys to overhear.

The Manager's smile returned, he paused for a moment as if calculating the interest rates. "The first week is on the house, after that please look out for your name on the duty roster."

Now it was Lewis who was smiling, this was exactly what they needed, a chance at a new life. One that involved beds, food and most importantly, a future they all could look forward to.

"I will have Mr Two Hands prepare a room for all of you at once."

Lewis had more than a few questions, but in the interest of good first impressions, he decided it best to leave it be for the time being.

He silently motioned for the boys to put the cutlery down and join him which took several attempts before they finally got the hint.

"Boys, this is The Manager, he is kind enough to let us stay." Lewis said whilst giving them each a firm nudge.

"Thank you" they both said sheepishly in unison.

Martin still had one hand on his cheek, which was turning a nasty shade of black and purple, forcing his eye shut. It was remarkable to see him in good spirits despite the obvious pain he must have been in. Martins other hand rested on the immaculate white desktop, leaving a perfect handprint of muck. Lewis suddenly realised just how dirty and smelly they must have all looked in comparison to The Manager.

He was so well kempt, clean shaven, with trimmed, gelled hair, even having minty fresh breath.

Lewis and the boys however looked like they had been stuck in the deep, dark jungles of the Amazon, with their ragged clothes and long bushy hair. Lewis had tried his best to keep them clean, but it proved to be an impossible task and over time they simply became so used to the smell that it stopped being an issue. He did ensure to keep his beard as short as possible, although this wasn't due to hygiene reasons, but rather remembering the man with the longest beard in the world died after tripping over it. Plus, he really didn't care for the amount of grey hair creeping in.

Ding, ding, ding

The Manager rang yet another, more petite bell in quick succession this time from behind the desk as the sound carried up one of several speaking tubes. This served to distract The Manager long enough for Lewis to wipe down the desk with his sleeve and raise his eyebrows at Martin.

"Your room will be ready in five minutes, if you wouldn't mind signing the guest book and then waiting at the bottom of the stairs. Mr Two-Hands will be down to greet you in due course."

Lewis gave The Manager a nod rather than a dirty handshake and proceeded to scribble his and the boy's names in the guest book which had been filled with previous entries. Lewis began to scan through the entries, but The Manager quickly slammed it shut and placed it underneath the desk before he could see anything of note.

Not wanting to cause any offence he ushered the boys towards the stairs as asked, walking past a row of long dormant elevators.

"Oh and do mind out for Stan and Ollie won't you" added The Manager. As the trio stopped and looked back with perplexed expressions. "they're quite harmless I assure you."

Lewis suddenly became aware of a rancid smell, reminiscent of leaving a bottle of baby formula in the hot sun for a week. No, it was more like the great stink the gathering carried with them, a tell-tale sign of approaching dead. Then came a set of low resonating growls, not a friendly sound at all but whenever is a growl truly friendly?

That's when Lewis saw them, two zombies stood in place, hidden in shadow as they shuffled slowly into the light. One was tall and thin, the other short and stout, both wearing dusty, moth-eaten suits. They had been crudely muzzled with what looked like chicken wire and oven mitts duct taped to their hands. Both Tom and Martin instantly recoiled in horror, hiding behind their dad, wishing they still had their formidable sticks.

"Quick, get a weapon!" Lewis called out to The Manager.

But instead, The Manager casually walked over to the bound zombies and gave them each a firm pat on the shoulder.

"Ha-ha, don't mind these two rascals, they're the help around here. Meet Stan and Ollie, they do all sorts from run a mop around, pulling heavy loads, hell they even generate a modest amount of electricity on our treadmills. Ollie's personal best is ten kilometres in five and a half hours, which is pretty decent given his medical condition."

"But they're zombies" said Lewis, stating the obvious.

"Oh, that's not an acceptable term we use around here I'm afraid, as its culturally insensitive." said The Manager, defending his former assailants. "I too was once ignorant to such matters."

"However, the vitally challenged, the living impaired, the undead community, individuals with pseudo-rigor mortis or teenagers are all acceptable terms. But never zombies as it defines them by their affliction, of which they have no control."

A zombie clutching his nether regions had now been bumped down to second on the weird-o-meter for the day. The sign wearing, waving zombie was now a pitiful third.

"But they're zom, I mean living impaired" said Lewis, trying his best to bite his tongue. "Surely, they are dangerous!"

If looks could kill, Lewis and his two sons would currently be pushing up daisies.

"I assure you sir, that these kind and gentle creatures are intelligent and contribute to the rebuilding of our society." The Manager had even gone to the trouble of placing a cross, the star of David and the Hebrew letter Chai around their necks, as he did not want them to miss out on heaven due to a technicality.

An awkward silence filled the room as the trio looked down guiltily at their shoes, not wanting to make eye contact with The Manager. Zombie Stan and Zombie Ollie's yellow, pus-filled eyes however were locked on to the new arrivals, with a look of primal hunger, but they remained steadfast for the time being.

Showing just how well trained they were.

What seemed like an eternity passed as they awkwardly waited in silence at the base of the stairs for this "Mr Two Hands."

"I do hope you all enjoy your stay" said The Manager, just to ramp up the guilt factor.

Martin placed both of his hands into his pockets and gave his little plastic duck a squeeze, causing it to let out a short and sharp squeak.

"And what was that young man?"

Martin shrugged his shoulders and continued to look down at his shoes, as The Manager and his vitally challenged colleagues glared at him.

"You wouldn't happen to have a duck in your pocket, would you?"

Martin cleared his throat. "Um, yes, we saw them outside and um, well."

The Manager stretched out his hand. "And do you often take things that don't belong to you?"

Lewis gave Martin a reassuring pat on the back. "Give it back to the gentleman please."

Martin reluctantly did as he was asked, removing the duck from his pocket, handing it back to the Manager as a single tear rolled down his bruised face.

Sorry, he didn't mean anything by it, he's just a kid, you know?" said Lewis.

The Manager took hold of the plastic duck and placed it into his jacket pocket. "Yes, well no harm done I suppose, just as long as there aren't any more sticky fingers from now on."

"No, I promise you it won't happen again."

Tom didn't dare open his mouth and said a little prayer in his head that his duck would remain silent.

"These aren't for playing with you know, they are a sophisticated security alarm system. Any unwelcome visitors step on these and the high-pitched squeaks will alert us" explained the Manager.

Lewis silently moved the boys closer to the base of the stairs, as a flickering light began to descend towards them. Signalling the arrival of the fabled Mr Two Hands who was also very well presented in a nice suit, minus a tie which instead dangled from his trouser pocket.

It was difficult to see his face in the dark stairwell, as the light cast from his lantern flickered wildly in all directions. But it was clear that he didn't have the friendliest of expressions.

"Alright you lot, I'm Hank-Two-Hands, I'll be showing you to your room." Hank did indeed have two hands as per his odd nickname.

The trio proceeded to follow him in utter silence up the winding staircase as both Zombie Stan and Zombie Ollie kept their well-trained eyes fixated on them. Martin could have sworn he saw them licking their grotesque lips in anticipation of a fresh meal.

There was an air of uncertainty about this place, a strange feeling lingered within these walls, but Lewis remained cautiously optimistic, despite the odd company The Manager kept and the poor first impression of one stolen duck.

The day had been long and enduring, taking as many twists and turns as this stairwell. Beginning with tins of dog food and Turkish Delight, then moving on to Dreadnought, a functional phone and ending with the possibility of real beds. Even the boys shook off the auspicious encounter, and looked up at their dad like he was some sort of superhero.

And in that moment, that's exactly how Lewis felt.

Hank-Two-Hands

It was one of Hank-Two-Hands many duties to keep the hotel well-lit without burning down as well as prepare rooms and greet guests where needed. For the most part he was a fast and diligent worker who contributed his fair share to the hotel. But there was just one problem, he was certifiably insane. Having mastered the act of pretending to be stable enough to carry on without being noticed.

After appropriating a substantial number of books from the local library, The Manager had taken inspiration from Leonardo Da Vinci, building a series of skybridges from rooftop to rooftop. This is when he and Hank-Two-Hands first met.

Initially The Manager thought he was in for the fight of his life upon crossing paths with the stranger who looked to be more beast than man. Hank-Two-Hands was this wild looking thing, with thick black matted hair, and a long beard that carried various bits of meals past. To say the Apocalypse had not been kind to him would be putting it mildly.

But The Manager was able to disarm his wild guest with some skilfully executed words, rather than resort to violence. At first, he considered asking the three "Walking dead questions, but couldn't seem to remember what the last one was.

"How many walkers have you killed? How many people have you killed? And how many jars of Nutella have you eaten?" Didn't quite sound right.

After giving the wild man food, clothing and a much-needed trim, it soon became apparent that Hank-Two-Hands had quite a bit to offer in terms of building and engineering knowledge. It didn't take much persuading to make Hank-Two-Hands second in command of the hotel and together they quickly were operational, beyond The Managers wildest dreams.

While The Manager had the mindset and vision for the hotel, he was somewhat lacking on the practical application front.

Whereas Hank-Two-Hands had been a skilled tradesman in his former life, able to apply his craft to just about anything. Truth be told The Manager wasn't always sure what his new friend was up to, but with the additions of gas-powered stoves, fire stoked boilers for warm water, speaking tubes and various pulley systems, he was more than happy to let Hank-Two-Hands go about his business.

Prior to Black Sunday Hank-Two-Hands had not only been a skilled tradesman but also a father to twins, a son and a daughter. But sadly, his daughter died on Black Sunday courtesy of a skinny and frighteningly fast zombie, that snatched her from her dad's two hands never to be seen again.

A month later his son caught his leg on a rusty nail, which didn't look too bad at first, but after a week his veins turned a deep shade of blue, bulging from the skin. By the time they found antibiotics it was too late as his son was simply too ill to carry on, succumbing to a blistering fever.

When the world was normal, he used to go home after a long day of work, and do things such as teach his kids how to mine an obsidian block with a diamond pickaxe in Minecraft. But after his children died, he became little more than an animal, losing his grip on reality, surviving on scraps and sleeping in a makeshift den. If it weren't for The Manager, then perhaps Hank-Two-Hands would still be out there to this very day.

But not even The Manager knew the true extent of his insanity which included but was not limited to hearing voices and seeing the ghostly apparitions of his children. These voices ranged from giving him instructions to outright calling him a madman.

"Shame on you!" he would call out. "I am your father and I will not have you call me names!"

Of course, the voices had a point, he was stark raving mad, perhaps not mad enough to write signs in his own excrement, but still very bizarre in his own right. Hank-Two-Hands had once thought himself to be the unluckiest man in the world and with good cause, but despite all his tragedies that title belonged to another man named Roy C. Sullivan.

Roy held the record for being struck by lightning and surviving an astounding seven times. Subsequently Roy died on Black Sunday of a self-inflicted gunshot wound, which was very unlucky indeed.

So, Hank-Two-Hands set about his new life at the hotel, keeping himself as busy as possible. For example, just before the desk bell rang three times to instruct him to prepare for their new arrivals, he had been on his hands and knees after bashing another poor soul's head in for a tin of food. Upon reflection it may seem unnecessary and violent, but to look at it from his point of view, this wasn't just any old tin of food, it was a tin of Branston baked beans!

Brushing off pinkish, grey brain matter, keeping the biggest chunks for later use, he claimed his prize. At this stage of the apocalypse, finding a tin of baked beans was the equivalent of winning the lottery after three roll overs. Now all he had to do was share the spoils with his ghostly companions before anyone became wise to his antics. Hank-Two-Hands tightly gripped the dented and gooey tin, practically tasting the thick orange sauce. His two hands remained calm and steady as if all this were second nature.

He glanced over at the poor soul who dared to previously possess the tin. She laid face down on what was once a very nice marble tiled kitchen floor, as blood flowed into the grooves like an evil river.

Blood was redder than he had once thought it to be, reminding him of raspberry-ripple sauce being drizzled across a freshly made ice cream. Although he was never too keen on raspberry-ripple sauce, it was always too sticky for his liking.

Hank-Two-Hands stood himself up, both of his knees creaked and cracked in doing so. He turned to face an overturned dining room table that somehow still had a tablecloth firmly clinging on. It was then two small ghostly faces appeared from around each side, staring intently with devious grins.

"Hey there kiddo's, who's hungry?"

Room 105

The lantern looked very old and heavy, like something from the 18th century. The glass was a Smokey white colour which glowed orange, while the metal handle was a rich black in contrast. Just looking at it made Lewis's arm ache, but Hank-Two-Hands seemed to carry it with ease, like he could do it with just one finger. The orange glow flickered along the dark hallway, light bouncing off the clean white walls, occasionally reflecting off a glass frame. Hank-Two-Hands led the way as the trio silently followed.

"So, um how comes they call you Hank-Two-Hands?" Lewis asked meekly, breaking the silence.

There was a sigh, the sort of sigh one does after having been asked the same question multiple times.

"Cause there's another bloke called Hank living here, on the ground floor" Hank-Two-Hands responded gruffly.

That sort of half explained the reasoning behind the unusual nick name, but if they were all going to be living together then Lewis simply had to know the full story.

"Oh, I see, so does the other Hank only have one hand in that case?"

Hank sighed again and turned towards Lewis. Even the boys could tell that their dad was poking the proverbial bear at this point. The dim light made Hank-Two-Hands look most imposing, despite being a good five inches shorter than Lewis.

"If you must know it's cause he's blind, but we don't judge on medical conditions round here, alright?"

Lewis just nodded with a befuddled expression and continued to the room without uttering another word. Hank-Two-Hands was running his fingertips along a long piece of string that ran the entire length of the hallway, acting as a guide to each door in the darkness. Coupled by a unique set of beads threaded through to help indicate room numbers. It was quite a clever little system they had created, adding to the list of many little things Lewis was quietly impressed by.

"Here we go, room one-oh-five."

Lewis had another flash back to his tarot card reading days. The number one-hundred and five if he remembered correctly was a sign of truth. It also meant something along the lines of stop pretending and start being yourself. Of course, Lewis didn't really believe any of that tarot stuff, he thought it was all utter nonsense. But in his defence, the girl he had learnt it for was very pretty.

Hank-Two-Hands proceeded to take out a comically large set of keys which seemed to make the loudest sound in the world. They weren't used to such loud things back in the muddy field, between the car engine and keys jangling it felt like their ear drums would implode at any given moment.

The door key-card readers had all stopped working long ago, having now been replaced with clunky but efficient padlocks, with Hank-Two-Hands performing a dangerous balancing act between the lantern and the lock.

"Did you want me to hold the light?" Lewis asked before Hank-Two-Hands quickly snapped at him.

"I got it, I got it!"

After a few failed attempts, the door swung open and they entered, the room was almost pitch black, except for the moonlight slipping through a gap between the thick curtains. The night sky had drawn in even sooner today, making their arrival to the hotel all the timelier. Lewis opened the curtains to allow more light which revealed two double beds, both clean and made up, as well as a small single sofa with additional bedding.

There were three "welcome bags" sat on one bed which was a very nice touch.

Opposite the beds was a small desk, upon which an identical looking lantern sat atop. Hank-Two-Hands proceeded to light this lantern using the flame from his.

"Right, as The Manager said, the first week is on the house, after that you need to earn your keep, yeah?"

Lewis and the boys were elated and nodded unconditionally to these terms. The room was a much welcome sight after spending the last couple of years squashed up in a three-man tent, in a soggy field.

"Right, well there's a welcome bag for each of you." he said, gesturing in their general direction.

If this were a film, this would have been the part were the concierge stood there awkwardly, hinting for a tip and that's exactly what Hank-Two-Hands did. But Lewis had nothing to offer him, nothing he wanted to part ways with at least. There was simply no chance he would give away the car keys or the partially charged phone. Regardless, Hank-Two-Hands just stood there, waiting with his palm outstretched.

Lewis waited a moment before moving in, shaking his hand.

"This is all very much appreciated" he said, hoping that would do the trick.

"Erm, right, well spose I best get going then" Hank-Two-Hands said, looking at his empty hand as if it were covered in sticky raspberry-ripple sauce.

"Well, there are instructions on how things work round here on the desk. Just remember we ain't liable for lost or damaged items." He threw a spare key onto the nearest bed and turned to leave the room.

"Thank you so much again! We really are" the door slammed shut, cutting Lewis off mid-sentence. "Grateful."

The boys celebrated with high five's and both began to jump up and down on the beds, Martin even seemed to forget about his poor face as the two of them literally jumped for joy. Lewis let them play and rummage through their welcome bags which each consisted of two bottles of water, an apple, a book, a small portion of dry cured meat, a wind-up torch, some ill-fitting clothes and a bar of soap. There was even some paper and crayons for the boys to enjoy.

Tom and Martin eventually settled down, getting under the covers and breathing a huge sigh of relief. The room reminded them of the ones they used to stay in at Butlins, clean and quite comfortable, miles better than that sodding tent. God how they hated that tent and that muddy field, if they had any say in the matter, they would never have left their home. After all it's where all their stuff was, books, toys and game consoles, just sitting there unloved and forgotten. Oh how they missed their game consoles, between them they had a Nintendo switch, a Nintendo Wii, an Xbox one, two laptops and a PS4.

Back in the tent they used to pretend they were playing Fortnite and they were the last two remaining in the battle royale.

"I'm a Fortnite pro, you're just a noob."

"No way I'm a noob, I'm much better than you!"

"What you talking bout bro, your just a rubbish no skin, I've got way more victories than you."

"Whatever, you had the battle pass!"

"Well, I ain't got that now, anyway shall we meet at Salty Springs? See what we can loot?"

"Yeah okay, then it's you versus me."

"It's always you versus me."

Then Lewis would usually have to intervene, stopping them from wondering off and generally being too loud.

But at the hotel, they were free to raise their voices within reason, to play and be kids again.

A small hand poked out from underneath a duvet. It was Tom's who had claimed the single sofa for himself.

"Quack."

He opened his hand to reveal a yellow plastic duck, complete with a little rainbow wig.

"Quack, quack."

Martin smiled and reached out towards the duck, but Tom quickly closed his hand tightly around it. Tom flung off the duvet and sat up at the edge of the sofa.

"It has to be a secret, you need to hide it somewhere safe, only play with it when we are in the room."

Martin thought about it for a moment, but quickly realised his brother was right on this occasion, it was best to keep it a secret.

"Thank you, I will hide him, keep him safe."

Tom loosened his grip and passed the duck to his brother. It was silly, but Tom could see that plastic bath toy really seemed to cheer Martin up, which in turn made him feel good, better than he had felt in a long time. Lewis watched Tom and Martin with an enormous sense of pride, it was clearly the right decision to come to the hotel.

He took the apple out of his welcome pack and took a big bite. It was a wonky looking apple, but it tasted amazing nonetheless, the juice was almost overpowering as it hit his taste buds. Lewis let out a content "mmm" and walked over to the desk, picking up the list of hotel rules which had all been written on an old-fashioned typewriter, numbered out with Roman numerals.

Lewis took another bite and read aloud the rules, crunching happily away all the while.

"Welcome to the Holiday Inn express Stevenage."

"To help you make the most of your stay, we simply ask that you please abide by our ten house rules."

I Breakfast is at 08:00, Lunch is at 13:00 and dinner is served at 18:00, all in the main hall. You will find a wind-up clock in your bedside cabinet, please be on time.

II Water rations will be handed out at breakfast each day so please use wisely.

III The duty roster is placed in the main hall and will rotate on a weekly basis. Please ensure you keep up to date with this.

IV We encourage you to make full use of the hotel, but please be mindful to keep the noise down due to gatherings.

V The library is in conference room one, the classroom is in conference room two, the town hall is in conference room three, and conference room four is strictly off limits.

VI The roof top garden is open for you to enjoy, but please refrain from disturbing the crops and water irrigation system.

VII When answering natures call, please use the buckets provided in room 110 on this floor, these are used as fertilizer for the garden. Once finished please attach the bucket to the pulley system outside the window and bring in clean buckets ready for the next person to use.

VIII Please ensure black out curtains are drawn when using any lighting, day or night.

IX Please refrain from leaving the hotel unattended unless permitted otherwise.

X Lastly and most importantly, do enjoy your stay, we are honoured to have you here.

"The Manager."

Lewis's attention suddenly turned towards the open curtains. Their window faced towards another hotel across the road, located on the other side of an empty car park. It was in this hotel a more sinister breed of the formally living dwelled, which had secretly been dubbed by The Manager simply as "Big'uns."

They could be observed through a powerful set of binoculars, seemingly staring right back at you, stood perfectly still, especially the biggest one.

Its theorised that a flock of flamingos could pick a T-Rex clean in under ninety seconds, but this particular gathering of Big'uns could do it in under sixty. Not that there were any T-Rex's wondering around, that would be ludicrous.

Lewis quickly scrambled to close the curtains, but it was too late, the light had caught the vigilant gaze of the largest and most aggressive Big'un. Standing close to seven foot tall, its spine unnaturally elongated. The Big'un had been in the gym when it turned, still sporting grey jogging bottoms and an army green shirt with a picture of the Hulk that read "The Beast Within."

This Big'un was their Alpha and under its command the gathering would emerge at night to hunt.

This gathering wasn't averse to eating their own kind as well as humans, in fact, the ringing of large brass bells had awoken the Big'uns. One by one they plucked the passing undead buffet off the street, eating them in a single sitting. The more of their own kind they devoured the more aggressive they became, the virus altering them even further. Causing horrible growths and deformities, their hunger now insatiable, never ending, always thinking of what they could consume next, but what they really craved were the fresh ones.

If it were not for the gym wear clad Alpha, they would have stormed the tasty humans hotel long ago. But the Alpha had taken charge with a series of grunts and displays of strength, and under its guidance they bided their time. Waiting until there were enough plump and juicy ones for the entire gathering to devour. The Alpha using its last remaining brain cells to plot their every move.

Its bloodshot, pus-filled gaze studied the human's hotel, memorising every inch of barbed wire, every entrance and exit, every possible weakness, within its rotten, infected brain. Every new arrival, every new security feature and of course, every departure.

Those humans never did get far thanks to the skilfully executed plans of the Alpha, but they were mere appetisers before the main course. Not a scrap went to waste of those tasty humans, they peeled back the skin while they were still raw and wriggling, popping their eyes like champagne corks. They even ate the fingernails like crisps and sucked the marrow from their bones, delicious stuff.

They waited for what seemed like an age, but with the addition of the trio, the time was finally right to strike. The Alpha's bloated, decaying tongue smacked against its lips as it bore a jagged tooth grin, maggots wriggling free, falling to the floor.

With a short, sharp grunt, it cleared its throat and forced a single syllable word.

"Soon" it uttered, "soon."

The Residents

In total there were twelve rooms in use by eighteen People at the hotel. Two of whom were classed as "Living impaired" or something to that extent. Lewis, Tom and Martin were the most recent to check in, giving a nice little boost to the residents numbers.

Prior to them, the latest addition was a lady by the name of Elinor who was a similar age to that of Lewis. She had been on her way north with her boyfriend before running into a large gathering. She arrived at the hotel alone, pale as a ghost and trembling. That was six months ago now.

Then there was Alec, an elderly gentleman who referred to himself as stoic. But most people who met him thought he was a bit of a knob. In any case there was no denying he was a dab hand in the communal gardens, growing all sorts of wonderful fruits and vegetables for everyone to enjoy.

The Patterson's, a lovely husband and wife couple shared a room. However, they both spoke with such thick Glaswegian accents that it was almost impossible to understand them. When the Manager first met them, he had asked them their first names several times but based on the unwritten rule of three, he simply smiled and said, "pleased to make your acquaintances, Mr and Mrs Patterson."

Hank, who also hand two hands but happened to be blind was placed in one of the disabled rooms on the ground floor. He hadn't always been blind, but after thoroughly disinfecting a room with undiluted bleach, he literally kicked the bucket, causing the liquid chemical to go directly into his eyes. He still maintains that one day his sonar, Daredevil like senses will kick in. That was nine months ago now.

Margery was a sweet, older lady, who had surprised everyone with her survival skills. Survival was in her blood as she was a direct descendant of one lieutenant Jack "Mad" Churchill, the only known British soldier in World War Two to have killed an enemy soldier with a longbow. Keen to keep the family tradition alive, Margery insisted on defending herself with both a medieval bow and a claymore sword.

Unfortunately, Margery had taken a bit of a shine to Hank-Two-Hands upon her arrival, which would ultimately become her undoing. Out in post-apocalyptic England, she had done rather well for herself, but within the confines of the hotel, Hank-Two-Hands had decorated the kitchen floor with her grey matter, and all for a tin of baked beans. The other residents were yet to become aware of her fate.

Zombie Stan and Zombie Ollie, the hotels resident undead ambassadors shared a room on the ground floor, tucked away in the northeast corner. The Manager liked to keep them around for manual labour purposes, plus they acted like guard dogs. They would snarl and growl at so much as a hint of another zombie passing within close proximity, giving the other residents ample warning. Their room was strictly off limits as anyone who saw inside would more than likely vomit on the spot. All the furniture had been removed bar the twin beds and the windows were boarded up tight. Excrement and bile littered the once royal blue carpet and a demonic looking baby-mobile hung from the ceiling. This consisted of various animal limbs, entrails and a woven bag of fresh lavender to help them relax and make the room smell marginally better. It did neither of those things.

The Darlings shared a room, their actual names being Reginald and Petunia Barclay who had once been wealthy socialites. But they called each other darling in their posh, Surrey based accents so much, that they simply became known as the Darlings. They liked using big words they didn't fully understand the meaning of, to sound more sophisticated in front of company.

"Darling, be a dear and pass me the water would you."

"But of course, darling, oh look it's from somewhere called Tesco."

"Oh, how quaint, you can practically taste the photosynthesis."

"Thank you darling."

"Most welcome Darling, mwah."

They claimed their money came from a self-built property management portfolio, but the reality was they stumbled across a waxy, yellow substance on the shores of Devon. It was ambergris,

70

more commonly known as wale vomit. They sold the "floating gold" for a small fortune and used the money to raise their social status, failing to mention where the money really came from as image was everything in their new world.

Avril, who was named after the pop, punk princess of the early noughties shared a room with her girlfriend known only as Red. Before the arrival of Tom and Martin, they had been the youngest guests of the hotel, both at the tender age of twenty-one. They were both anti-establishment vegans and had caused havoc with their extinction rebellion protests, causing severe delays to the general public and costing the average taxpayer hundreds of thousands of pounds in the process. Then with a smug look and new "edgy" photos for their Instagram accounts, they would head home using public transport and whack the central heating up to a toasty twenty-eight degrees Celsius. These days they were more than happy to be working for "The Man."

Darren was the most reclusive and least known about within the hotel. Being thirty something with a decent physique, only emerging from his room to get breakfast and water rations each day, then head out on duty before finally retiring back to the privacy of his room. Darren had travelled a couple of hundred miles to the hotel on horseback, just like in the 1971 song by the band formally known as America, on a horse with no name. The horse's name was actually Frank.

Darren usually kept his distance from people to look tough and show some bravado. However, the reality was to keep others from discovering he suffered from a severe case of Anatidaephobia. The fear that at any given point, somewhere in the world, a duck or goose may be watching you. Which was obviously only made worse when it was discovered birds were infecting the entire planet. No one had ever seen him at dinner and nor would they any time soon, just in case a sinister fowl was lurking close by.

Lastly and by no means least, Hank-Two-Hands and The Manager, whose real name remained a mystery to the other guests made eighteen.

Together they were the ragtag bunch that made up the very fabric of the hotel.

Well seventeen now.

Poor Margery.

Elinor

Elinor was tall and slender, with wavy, mousey brown hair and piercing blue eyes. Lewis was amazed by how good she looked and how she was able to take pride in her appearance despite the world falling apart around her. She looked like she belonged in a Michael Bay movie, the kind where there are loads of explosions and everyone runs for their lives, but somehow still look perfect.

Once Lewis saw her, he quickly grew self-conscious and made arrangements for himself and the boys to have a wash and get a haircut. Not that he thought he had a chance with her or anything, she probably wasn't into single dads who looked like they just crawled out from a ditch. But still, he wanted to look nice, just in case.

Getting clean was like spending the day at one of those fancy pamper spas, being poked and prodded as Mrs Patterson offered to give him a much-needed makeover. She even gave him a splash of Poundland's finest aftershave which stung his bramble vine cut scrapes like hell. The results were worth the effort though as Lewis was almost unable to recognise the man staring back at him in the mirror. It felt amazing just to be clean again, which had the desired effect, gaining the attention of the lovely Elinor.

She was more than just a pretty face though; she was smart and tougher than old boots. Her journey to the hotel hadn't been pleasant by any means, in fact it was the hardest thing she had ever done. But she was here, still standing and proving her worth amongst the men who wanted to play hotel.

The male residents were simple creatures, ones of habit and routine, in Elinor's opinion they were easier to work out than any zombie. This is why she took so much pride in her appearance, after all it wasn't easy staying clean in the apocalypse. But thanks to a hidden stash of baby wipes, Elinor kept her skin clean and always made sure her hair was thoroughly brushed. These attributes combined with a well-placed hand touch and men would fall over themselves to help her anyway possible. An extra bottle of water at breakfast, some goodies from a supply run, swapping the duty rota around, you name it. It may sound a bit on the manipulative side, but it was no worse than The Manager sending people out on supply runs in return for staying at "his" hotel.

Elinor didn't intend to stay though, after all why stay put when there is a whole world to see beyond these beige walls. For the past six months she had been acquiring enough items to make it on her own, out there in the real world, far away from what she considered to be hotel nonsense. She even thought about making a break for it when she heard about Darren's horse. Her eyes lit up when she saw the stallion, Frank that was, not Darren.

With her supplies bolstered and a permanently borrowed horse, she could go north, far away from the living and the dead and just live out her life in peace. But it didn't take the group long to persuade Darren to part ways with his horse, opting to have it as a meal rather than a means of transportation. So, unless another means of travel miraculously showed up, she was stuck here for the foreseeable future.

That's when Lewis arrived, there was something about him that intrigued her and it wasn't just the car key concealed in his pocket. Sure, he looked rough as hell, but who wouldn't having lived out in a field for two years. He had a way about him, kind and considerate, he wasn't hardened by the apocalypse to the point of being standoffish. Lewis had made sure to stay down to earth for the sake of his boys and that was something Elinor could respect.

She didn't have any kids of her own, it never really occurred to her as she was always too busy enjoying her own life. Not that she didn't like kids, but bringing them to a nightclub wasn't exactly ideal, let alone raising them in the apocalypse. Regardless, Elinor found herself gravitating towards him.

At first she gave Lewis and his boys space when they first arrived, as she could remember how daunting the first few days at the hotel could be. All those new living faces, crowding you, full of questions, judging you and then there was Zombie Stan and Zombie Ollie to content with.

After a couple of days Elinor properly introduced herself, choosing to sit with them at dinner. That evening the menu consisted of boiled rice, some powdered custard and beer, actual beer. Nothing fancy, little bottles of Bière Continentale that held a mere 2.8% alcoholic volume, but still some libations were a great way to break the ice. Elinor and Lewis grew close very quickly, but even so she held back from telling him certain aspects of her life before the hotel. She wasn't ready for that just yet.

Elinor knew she was very fortunate to have a new friend in Lewis, feeling slightly optimistic for the first time in a long time. With roof top chilled Bière Continentale in their hands, they made a toast for the future, whatever it may hold.

Tell Me Lies

The ground shook and exploded into thousands of fragmented pieces, each blow to the surface greater than the previous. The ground churned and spewed into the air, revealing a layer of bland, yet rich dark soil as the earth was being forced back to its once natural state. Exhausted Lewis wiped the sweat from his brow, his lungs working hard to pull oxygen into his body. Then he saw it, his eyes widened with panic as he realised the danger he was about to be in. He was going to be late dropping the boys off for class.

A week had passed as the trio had gotten to know the ins and outs of the hotel. On their second day they were asked to attend the town hall for a welcome meeting. It was slightly embarrassing for the boys to be the centre of attention, but Hank-Two-Hands had taken a bit of a shine to them. Joking around with them both and generally making sure they were well looked after. Lewis even managed to impress the hotels second in command, showing Hank-Two-Hands how to make an effective snare trap, in return for his generosity.

"That's a nasty bruise you got kiddo, lets visit the first aid room for something to help with that" said Hank-Two-Hands to Martin.

With his dad's approval off they went, returning with an instant cool pack and a lollipop for each of the boys. Everyone cooed over the new arrivals and barraged them with a million questions ranging from "What is it like out there, did you see any other survivors, did you see naked zombies walking around?" the latter question asked by Avril who had a morbid desire to set up Zombie Stan and Zombie Ollie with undead dates.

Lewis gained even more attention once he was washed and cleaned, seemingly having a certain amount of appeal when it came to the fairer sex.

Perhaps this was down to solely taking care of two boys in a zombie infested world, but more than likely it was simply due to a lack of other options. This caused a bit of a grumble amongst the hotels married residents, but once they saw how quickly he and Elinor bonded their worries quickly subsided.

All in all, everyone seemed pleasant enough and pulled their weight very well. Lewis had gained a lot of respect in a short time for The Manager and his well-oiled machine. They had even gotten used to the idea of a vitally challenged workforce as long as the proper precautions were taken.

The Manager was telling the truth when he said Zombie Stan and Zombie ollie pulled their weight. They charged batteries and other portable devices on modified treadmills, pushed trolleys to and from various destinations. They even mopped the reception floor with some gentle coaxing. At the end of each day, they were guided back into their shared room and given something to eat as a reward. Lewis wasn't exactly sure what they were fed but it was safe to assume it wasn't anything off the vegetarian menu.

Once Tom and Martin learned that things could be charged, they asked their dad to charge the phone for them, but Lewis held off, not wanting to share it just yet, much to the boy's disappointment.

Each day breakfast was at eight in the morning as specified, which mostly consisted of baked beans, spam and bottled water. Pretty much if it was in a tin, then it was on the menu. Lunch was a bit different in the sense that hardly anyone attended, as everyone just seemed too busy with their duties. Plus, they all knew it would help stretch the food rations a little further.

Finally, dinner was something else, actual meat with a side of potatoes and fresh sweetcorn. Lewis couldn't help being a little sceptical though, wondering if this was all for show. Perhaps this was all just to impress the new arrivals, but over the course of their first week the food didn't drop in size nor quality.

Halfway through their first week Tom spotted a tin of Quality Street chocolates just sitting on a side table, but upon opening, he was disappointed to find a rubbish old sewing kit instead.

At dinner no one questioned where the "fresh" meat came from, but they all knew it was more than likely rat or squirrel meat and what remained of Frank the horse. But as long as it wasn't potentially infected bird, then they were more than happy to tuck in. Each night that week they went back to their room with full bellies and read books from the library, formally known as conference room one.

Still the boys pestered their dad to charge the phone.

"I will get it charged up for you, just as soon as I'm out on duty." The boys sulked but knew they had no choice in the matter and went back to playing with their rainbow wigged duck who they decided to name Sebastian.

As for Dreadnought, on their first night Lewis broke rule number nine, sneaking out of the hotel to move it. It wasn't too difficult, he just waited until everyone was asleep and with a quick shimmy down a drainpipe directly outside their window, he was soon on the ground below. Lewis put the car into neutral and released the handbrake, slowly but surely, pushing the heavy car into a nearby underpass, placing it under some tarpaulin and cardboard boxes. Thankfully, there weren't any gatherings that night, but there was an ever-watchful Big'un following his every movement.

Getting back into the hotel was a bit trickier than it was getting out. Climbing back up the drainpipe took all of his upper body strength, like taking on the wall on Ninja warrior. Except the fall would be cushioned by squeaking bath ducks rather than a heated swimming pool.

Lewis didn't tell the boys, but he discreetly sliced into the base of Sebastian the duck with the sharpest knife he could find. Placing the car key inside, and sealing it back up by melting the plastic with the lanterns flame. The boys didn't seem to notice Sebastian's operational scar, or the slight difference in weight.

Each night Martin would hide it behind the U-bend of the toilet, unaware of what he was really concealing. Lewis didn't know why he hadn't told anyone else about the car yet, but that nagging voice kept him from mentioning it to the others for now. He supposed it was a plan B if needed, perhaps one day he would tell The Manager about it, just not right away. Of course, the boys had wanted to tell everyone how they arrived in a super sporty car, but Lewis instructed them to not say a word, not until they could fully trust their new neighbours.

Martin felt as if he might burst with such a big secret but didn't want to disappoint his dad and promised to keep his lips sealed.

The duty roster was on a big chalk board and placed in the main hall just as stated within the hotel rules, which was rotated on a weekly basis. Lewis's first assignment was one of the more pleasant duties, to help him get into the swing of things.

Allotment and water duty: Lewis, Alec, Elinor and the Patterson's, Mr and Mrs.

Construction and security: The Darlings, Mr and Mrs, Avril, Stan and Ollie.

Supply run: Darren and Red.

Operations: The Manager and Hank-Two-Hands.

Of course, the rota for operations remained the same each week, strictly allocated to the top brass.

Margery had been excused for the week as she was feeling under the weather, or at least that is what Hank-Two-Hands had informed The Manager. While Blind Hank had been assigned to tutoring the kids five days a week, giving them some semblance of normality.

It was a fair system that worked well. Obviously there were people who would rather be digging in the garden then having to do supply runs, dicing with the undead. But for the most part people supported one another and got on with it. Keep calm and carry on was the tried-and-true motto of the hotel, that and try not to get eaten.

Martin and Tom on the other hand were not so keen when they found out they would be spending each day with Blind Hank sat in a classroom picking up where they had left off in regular school. Blind Hank had little to contribute physically, but his mind, now that was a vital asset for the hotel. He had been bored silly since the bleach incident, but still insisted The Manager set up a classroom in one of the spare conference rooms.

"Education isn't a privilege, it's a necessity and a classroom will be of use I assure you." He informed The Manager repeatedly before finally being allowed to set up shop. The classroom sat unused and unloved until the boys arrived, but now it could be used, much to the boy's chagrin.

"Dammit" said Lewis just audible enough for anyone within earshot as he caught a glance at his new Poundland wristwatch. He had been keen to get a head start in the gardens on his first day, wanting to make a good impression once more. He was due to drop the boys off in just five minutes and get them signed in, which may have seemed like plenty of time to most people. But Lewis knew his boys weren't the quickest when it came to getting ready.

Filthy and covered in mud from digging away underneath the plastic sheets of a crudely made pergola, he dropped his shovel and moved quickly to go meet them. Stopping in his tracks, he knew if he didn't pack his tools away neatly, the other residents would most likely report this behaviour to the highest authority in the land. In this case not The Manager but instead one of the longest tenured guests of the hotel, Alec.

Alec was happiest when sat in his makeshift castle, comprising of old pallets and corrugated plastic sheets. He proudly sat surveying his small kingdom of compost and vegetable plots. This wasn't just a job for him, this was a place where his world made sense. The Manager may run the hotel but up here, Alec's word was final, for he was King of the allotments!

Quickly tidying his tools away, Lewis headed down the stairwell towards the first floor, failing to spot the trail of muddy footprints left behind him. As he entered room one-oh-five, it became apparent no one was there, unless the boys had really upped their hide and seek game, then they had already left.

Lewis locked up the room and proceeded to head down one more flight of stairs, making his way over to the classroom. Upon opening the doors, he saw both Martin and Tom sat at a table chatting with Hank-Two-Hands.

"Everything alright boys?" he asked to which they both nodded and immediately turned their attention back to the hotels second in command.

"Then what did you do?" asked Martin.

"Yeah, finish the story please" Tom pleaded.

"Well as I was saying, it was me and twenty of the most blood thirsty living impaired brutes you'd ever seen, nasty looking ones with snarling teeth and blood red eyes, that glowed in the dark. They came at me from all directions and honestly, I thought I was a goner."

The boys were wide eyed, engrossed in the story, for a moment even Lewis was captivated.

"Then I remembered about the fire extinguisher on me flatbed truck, I grabbed it quick as a flash and squeezed the handle." Martin let out and audible gasp and inched closer.

"Blinded the lot of 'em and escaped in the ruckus, you know what I did next?"

"No, tell us!" the boys asked in unison.

Hank-Two-Hands leant in and whispered for dramatic effect. "I got in my van and drove into the scaffolding supports, squashed the lot of'em flat! Turned them all into nothing more than raspberry-ripple sauce!"

The boys were flabbergasted; it was a much cooler story then lobbing tins of dog food at zombies it had to be said.

"Anyway, that's enough stories for now, you both got some learning to do" he said, giving Lewis a sly wink and left the room.

Lewis had to give the boys some credit, they were both clean, looked halfway decent, even if their clothes were a little non-matching. They even brought some water and an apple each, looking eager to learn.

"Are you two going to be okay in here while I'm on duty?" Lewis asked knowing he had left them on many other previous occasions in far worse circumstances.

"We will be fine, have fun at work" said Tom as Martin nodded in agreement. His cheek was a horrid shade of blueish purple, with a yellowish brown hugh. As bad as it looked, it was starting to look a bit better.

Martin had been very brave throughout the whole ordeal.

"Thanks boys, if you need anything come to the roof and find me."

The boys reassured him they would, and went back to sorting out their paper and pencils, trying their best to look like good students.

Hank-Two-Hands poked his head back into the room and with a single look beckoned Lewis to have a discreet word with him. Lewis was confused and assumed he must have been in trouble for not tidying his tools away properly, but this would not be the case.

He entered the silent hallway, shutting the door behind him as Hank-Two-Hands just stood there with a look of concern on his face.

Lewis knew it had to be something more serious, perhaps Alec had taken a disliking to his early start. God only knew what the punishment would be, perhaps this would be the final straw, making Alec snap, burning the entire place to the ground with Molotov cocktails, fermented from hotel grown potatoes.

"What's up?" Lewis asked trying his best to sound casual.

"I'm afraid their teacher won't be in today; he's feeling a little under the weather."

Tell me lies, tell me sweet little lies, Oh, no, no you can't disguise.

The instantly recognisable tones of 1987's little lies by Fleetwood Mac echoed down the halls, as The Manager walked past with an old-fashioned cassette player on his way to the front desk. He placed it down on the counter and busied himself with some hand drawn blueprints. It was nice to hear actual music, even if it was terribly outdated.

"Oh, I see, so um, can I take them on duty with me or?" Lewis asked.

Hank-Two-Hands kept his back against the wall and glanced past Lewis towards the classroom. "Tell you what, I can look after them."

Lewis was hesitant, but also still keen to keep everyone happy with him for the time being. Plus, the boys seemed to quite like Mr Two-Hands.

"I got a B in my English GCSE's, so I know the difference between there, their and they're, just listen to this." Hank-Two-Hands cleared his throat and looked straight up towards the ceiling as if mentally preparing to retrieve a long dormant memory.

"The formally living are over there, their limbs have fallen off, they're going to eat us. Ahh, see I told you, I know my stuff!"

Hank-Two-Hands was most convincing in his pitch to be the boy's substitute teacher, even if his examples of grammar were a little on the odd side.

"See, I'm sure I can keep them out of trouble for ya. But I don't do none of that religion nonsense yeah. I mean do people still really believe that stuff?"

Lewis wasn't a religious man himself, but if anyone had asked him a few years ago if he believed in zombies, his answer would have been a firm no. So perhaps there was more to religion than he had previously considered, but in the interest of keeping the peace he simply didn't answer the question. Which was just as well, as Hank-Two-Hands went off on a bit of a tangent.

"I mean, take the little drummer boy yeah, so Mary who is exhausted and just gotten her baby to sleep, is then approached by a young man who thinks to himself, you know what this girl needs is a bloody drum solo! Anyway, what was I saying? Oh yeah so, I can teach them no problem at all, whatcha say?"

Lewis couldn't help but think for a man who was so anti religion, Hank-Two-Hands seemed to know an awful lot on the subject, regardless it didn't take long for Lewis to take him up on the offer.

He opened the door slightly and took one more glance at the boys, before extending his hand towards their substitute teacher for the day.

Hank-Two-Hands oddly hesitated for a moment, before discreetly wiping his hands on the back of his jacket. Then gripped Lewis's in a strong, manly handshake, the type of handshake you really had to brace yourself for. Lewis thanked him once more as the two parted ways and set about their duties for the day. It was such a relief to be able to talk to, and trust another grown up.

But had Lewis glanced back just once more, then perhaps he would have noticed the smudge of fresh blood left on the wall by Hank-Two-Hands. Perhaps he would have noticed the distinct telltale signs of blood hastily wiped down the back of his jacket. But unfortunately, he didn't notice and as of that moment, Hank-Two-Hands was now the only Hank residing at the hotel.

Just nobody else knew it yet.

The residents were now down to sixteen.

Alpha

As Lewis finally made his way back up to the rooftop garden he was greeted by the others.

"Sorry I'm late, I had to drop the kids off at class."

Everyone gave an understanding nod and went back to work except for Alec who gave a disapproving glare, which Lewis chose to ignore.

After about half an hour of hard manual labour it became apparent that this wasn't a simple chore for these people, this was garden warfare. One bad harvest could lead to many hungry bellies, which simply would not do. Alec knew his stuff too and these people fell in line like his cauliflower soldiers. Alec lived by three simple rules: no hosepipes, no rubbish and no mercy!

The rooftop garden was well organised, with raised plant beds, full of various crops. Unfortunately for Lewis, there was a dedicated section for onions and Garlic, which he was more than keen to avoid. Several sheds and greenhouses had been constructed, all acquired from the local B&Q. All topped off with netting that ran overhead, covering the edges of the roof to prevent any infected birds from getting in, which seemed to work a treat.

The netting had already been in place long before the apocalypse, built to deter pigeons from nesting in the various air ducts that ran across the rooftop. Never was it imagined that one day the netting would be used to fend off the decaying remains of infected birds, but needs must.

It was obvious that a lot of work had gone into getting these materials here, which Lewis couldn't help but admire.

The next few hours were quite uneventful, as Lewis paired up with Elinor, rotating soil, learning how to convert human waste into fertilizer, which was just as romantic as it sounded. Alec oversaw things while the Patterson's went about various plant-based business.

"New bloke, move these pallets" Alec commanded.

"What's the magic word?" Elinor quickly chimed in.

Alec was clearly keen to assert some sort of dominance over what he considered to be his new lacky. But didn't quite know what to do when challenged by the opposite sex as it made him feel awkward and flustered.

"Please, I suppose."

"There, isn't that much nicer, Lewis and I would be more than happy to help out" she said with a wink, directed towards Lewis.

Alec grumbled and went back to sipping from a flask he kept concealed on his person, the contents of which were a mystery, but it was a fair bet it wasn't water. Time passed quickly as lunch time soon rolled around, but everyone was more than happy to stay up on the roof and enjoy the brisk air. After all it was no good being cooped up indoors all-day, plus a little vitamin D was always welcome. Even if the sun was obstructed by thick grey, stubborn ash clouds.

Lewis tidied his tools away, wiped off his boots along the edge of the wall and was about to head back downstairs to check on the boys, when Elinor gently tapped him on the shoulder.

"Off so soon?" she asked.

She brushed away a thick layer of ash at the edge of the roof and clapped her hands, which was like banging two chalkboard erasers together. A dark cloud hung in the air for a moment, dispersing with the gentle breeze. She then sat down and patted an empty space beside her invitingly.

Lewis knew the responsible thing was to go downstairs but reasoned with himself that an extra five minutes wouldn't do any harm and gladly sat beside her. A cold wind picked up, but after a couple of harsh winters in a cheap tent for protection against the elements, Lewis's skin had hardened to such things.

"So, are the boys enjoying life in the hotel?" asked Elinor, wrapping her arms around her waist for extra warmth.

"They love it here, they don't even mind having to share a room with me."

Elinor giggled coquettishly, it was the sort of cliché giggle accompanied by a well-placed hair stroke they used to do in films. Lewis didn't notice though, he wasn't used to girls flirting with him. Not that he wasn't good looking, no Brad Pitt admittedly, but still decent in his own right. The two chatted for much longer than five

86

minutes as Elinor subtly placed her hand on his knee, this he did notice. After two years without intimate contact the effect was instantaneous and embarrassingly difficult to conceal.

Lewis felt a sudden rush of blood to his face, luckily the cold wind brought out the red in his cheeks, masking his embarrassment. There was no denying there was an attraction, but he wasn't sure if he wanted this in his life right now. After all things were only just starting to look up, in his case quite literally, but the boys had to be placed first.

Elinor was somewhat of a mind reader and could tell he was conflicted. "It's okay to want things just for you. You've had it rough, so I can understand having your guard up, so no need to rush anything okay?"

It was hard to deny there was a connection, but from sitting at breakfast and dinner together to something more romantic was a big leap. If things turned sour, it would be impossible to avoid each other within the confines of the hotel. Just going to the library, they bumped into each other reaching for the last Deadpool graphic novel.

Quickly realising that they shared a love of comic book films and reminisced about the time Avengers End Game had come out in cinemas, talking about how excited they had been to see it. In a strange way movies reminded Elinor of her hometown of Brighton.

Cineworld Brighton had been where Elinor stayed after Black Sunday with her then boyfriend, long before she travelled north to the hotel. There had been plenty of vacuum sealed hotdogs, stale popcorn, sweets and Nacho's to keep them going at first, but it didn't last forever. Elinor hadn't told anyone why she left, other than the usual "just trying to survive" story that everyone seemed to have, but the reality was far more harrowing.

Elinor was born and raised in Brighton where she lived with her boyfriend of three years called Hugh. They had stuck it out as long as possible down south, making a decent go off it at the cinema and eventually moved onto the pier where they became quite skilled fishermen. But as with all good things it came to an end once a gathering had caught their scent.

This gathering caught them by surprise, emerging from the sea like an undead version of the Little Mermaid. They were all so fat and bloated from the cold, salty waters, bluey green in colour, some even bore large shark bite marks. Elinor was always prepared though, having two rucksacks packed and ready to go at a moment's notice as they made a run for it. The bloated gathering didn't fare well against the steep incline towards the train station, as Elinor and Hugh were able to shake them off with ease.

Hugh suggested travelling north, as far north as John O'Groats, a village near Dunnet Head, the northernmost point of Great Britain, hoping the cold weather would deter any undesirables. Maybe from there they would find an island to start from scratch, making a permanent home for themselves. But they only made it as far north as the A1 motorway, just twenty-two miles north of London when they ran into a gathering of huge, grotesque zombies, the likes of which they had never seen before.

These ones almost seemed to be organised, working as a cohesive unit. Led by a huge brute, wearing grey jogging bottoms and an army green shirt, with a picture of the Hulk.

Hugh had been mobbed by the gathering, tearing him limb from limb in mere seconds, while Elinor made a break for it. There was nothing she could have done, still, she felt pretty lousy about leaving him.

Elinor spent days, weeks crying over Hugh, until she realised there weren't enough tears in the world. As cruel as it sounded, grieving wouldn't make any difference and deep down, she knew that Hugh would have wanted her to make the most of her life. For her the hotel was only a pit stop as far as she was concerned, a place where she could heal her emotional wounds.

Elinor hadn't expected to like anyone else, especially not so soon. She didn't know if it was just a physical thing she was looking for, or something more than that. Either way Lewis hadn't factored into her plans and suddenly she noticed that he was looking at her, like he wanted nothing more in the world than to kiss her. Lewis leant in slowly wondering if he had totally misread the situation and was very aware that the Patterson's and Alec would all be watching.

Even the smell of the communal waste buckets weren't enough to spoil the moment though, as much to his surprise Elinor also closed her eyes and leant in.

They may have only known one another for just a week but it just felt right. Lewis closed his eyes with anticipation, ready to press his lips against hers when they were both startled by a blood curdling scream from the ground below.

It was Red and Darren, who were hobbling along at a frantic pace towards the hotel. The Patterson's, Mr and Mrs joined Lewis and Elinor at the edge of the rooftop to see what was happening, all mindful not to disturb the netting, lest they receive a severe tongue lashing from Alec.

The romance was well and truly gone.

"Oi you lazy lot, there is work to be done here" Alec called out.

Clearly, he hadn't heard the scream as he wiped spittle from his grey whiskers.

"Do I need to tell The Manager about this?" He was met with silence as the foursome kept their backs towards him, desperately trying to see what all the commotion was.

"Well, is anyone of you lot gonna answer me or what?"

"Oh do shut up! Elinor snapped. "Can't you see they need help!"

Scorned, Alec reluctantly joined them at the ledge. "Blimey, what they doing going that way round?"

Red and Darren were approaching the main entrance of the hotel rather than the side fire exit that was used to sneak in and out. It was hard to tell if they were hurt or not, as Darren had a long, dirty looking cloak wrapped around him, but he appeared to be supporting Red's weight as she dragged her feet alongside him.

Red was a good foot shorter than Darren, always wearing her trademark red hoodie with black stripes, making it easy to spot her from a distance.

"You guys okay? Lewis called out before receiving a stiff elbow to his side from Alec.

"Keep your bloody voice down will ya, no telling what's out there!" Alec was right, as difficult as it was, they all had to remain quiet. The best thing they could do now was run downstairs and let them in before things escalated.

"I'll go" said Lewis, springing into action, Elinor didn't need an invitation, she was already behind him, even managing to pick up a pitchfork just in case. They thudded down the stairwell together, as a surge of adrenaline gave them a much-needed boost. Five flights of stairs may not sound like much, but the twists and turns slowed them down, making them work for every breath. At last, they reached the ground floor and flung open the reception double doors, slamming them into the walls with an almighty bang. Leaving dirty, blackened dents for good measure.

The Manager had been caught off guard, giving him a severe fright.

"Excuse me!" he bellowed. "What exactly do you think you are doing?"

Obviously, he was not aware of the situation, as Red's previous scream had been drowned out by his cassette player, which was currently playing Queen's 1980 mega hit, Another one bites the dust.

"It's Darren and Red, they need our help!" said Elinor between sharp breaths. "They're outside the main entrance, we have to let them in, quickly!"

The Manager shot them a somewhat bemused and dismissive look. "Well, that's quite preposterous I'm afraid as Darren of all people knows better than to use the main entrance when on duty."

Suddenly the main bell rang; once, twice, three times.

"Another one bites the dust, another one bites the dust." Freddie Mercury still had an impeccable sense of timing it would appear.

Lewis and Elinor were now the ones shooting The Manager looks, looks of the utter most urgency.

"Well, if you two will excuse me we appear to have guests."

The Manager casually walked over to the door, making sure to take his time, just to prove a point. He was the one in charge here and would not be dictated to by anyone else, certainly not guests whom he had allowed the privilege to stay at his hotel.

Elinor readied her pitchfork whilst Lewis was now brandishing a barstool, even if he wasn't quite sure how he would use it. The Manager released the top deadbolt, followed by the bottom one, lastly removing a metal railing threaded through the double door handles.

Zombie Stan and Zombie Ollie shuffled into the reception area, alarmingly they had managed to evade Avril and the Darlings Mr and Mrs.

They both began to resonate a low growl, reminiscent of a bad-tempered crocodile. Lewis noticed this and remembered what The Manager had said about the undead duo, the Guard dogs had the scent of something they did not like at all.

"Wait, maybe you shouldn't open the doors," said Lewis.

Elinor gave him a look of disbelief, in that instant she wondered how she could have let herself like someone who could be so callous. But it was too late, as The Manager opened the doors and in shuffled a wide shouldered, cloaked figure, dragging beside him a clearly injured party wearing Reds distinctive hoodie. Lewis was surprised by just how relaxed the Manager seemed to be, not even having a weapon of sorts to defend himself from rogue living impaired.

"You two know better than to come around the front of house and was it really necessary to ring the bell like that?" The Manager asked while applying the deadbolts back into position, his voice lacking any sign of empathy.

Zombie Stan and Zombie Ollie were now almost frantic, desperate to remove their restraints and get at the cloaked figure, but like well trained dogs they kept their distance until given the command. It was clear something was terribly wrong as Darren and Red just stood there, in the middle of reception, motionless and silent.

"Stop!" Lewis barked at The Manager before he could thread the metal railing back through the door handles. "Something isn't right."

The Manager stopped dead in his tracks, as the room went uncomfortably quiet, no one dared move or even breathe. Darren and Red had brought in with them an almighty stench that quickly filled the room, bringing everyone to the edge of retching. There was no mistaking it, it was just like the great stink a gathering carried with them. Even in comparison, Zombie Stan and Zombie Ollie's room smelt quite pleasant when pitted against this, not by much though.

The Manager was just about to reiterate that he was the one in charge here and not Lewis, but there was no denying something was indeed wrong. The Manager stepped forward towards Red, his hand outstretched just a few inches from her limp shoulder. The back of Reds head was caked in fresh blood, but it was difficult to tell just how much she was bleeding as her dark hair masked it well.

Elinor stifled a scream, clasping her hands over her mouth as she noticed a pool of reddish-black gunk dripping from underneath Darren's cloak.

"Red, my dear are you okay?" asked The Manager with a nervous tremble.

Red let out a low moan, she was semi-conscious and trying to whisper something as The Manager slowly leant in closer to hear just exactly what she was saying.

"Ru... Ru...Ru..."

"What is it Red? What are you trying to say?"

"Run... and tell ... Av, Av, tell her I love her."

Everybody in the room apart from Zombie Stan and Zombie Ollie were frozen to the spot, like an old wild west stand-off. The vitally challenged duo were snarling, foaming at the mouth, ready to defend their turf at a moment's notice.

"Darren let's get her to the first aid room and then I want you to tell me exactly what happened," instructed the Manager.

But without warning the filthy cloak was flung off with one grotesque, elongated arm, revealing the Alpha Big'un in all its undead glory.

"Ours" it growled, much to everyone's shock and dismay.

In an instant Elinor recognised those dirty jogging bottoms and army green Hulk t-shirt, transporting her back to the night she lost Hugh. It was the very same brute that had torn him limb from limb as she fled into the darkness. A wave of emotion came over her as she fought back the tears, bracing herself for the battle ahead.

To everyone's horror, the Alpha twisted Red's neck with a sickening snap that echoed off the clean white walls and discarded her lifeless body across the room. It could come back with its gathering to devourer her later, once it had cleared out the hotel of all those lively, delicious humans. Red crashed into Zombie Stan and Zombie Ollie, toppling them over like bowling pins. Any undead assistance was now out of the equation as they lay there, both stunned and semi-conscious.

The Big'un was even bigger than observing him through binoculars had led The Manager to believe. It's contorted and misshapen body, hulking over him, much like its shirt implied. The rancid smell came from entrails that it wore around its neck, like a ghastly equivalent to the town mayor's golden chain. Its skin a mix of dull grey with splashes of gangrene and purple varicose veins, its stomach horribly distended.

The Alpha lunged for The Manager, looking to tear his arm clean off, but slipped in the puddle of reddish-black goo. It slid across the marble floor like demonic dancing on ice, crashing to the floor in a heap.

The Manager used this opportunity to get the hell out of its way, moving quickly to the other side of the room, luckily for him those knock off converse shoes still had some life left in them.

The Alpha quickly regained its footing and took aim at Elinor as it roared towards her with murderous intent.

"Ours!"

Elinor readied her pitchfork, turned her head away and shut her eyes, preparing for the worst, but quick as a flash Lewis stepped in with the barstool like a heroic lion tamer. The Alpha stopped in its tracks, seemingly amused as it displayed a twisted smirk and tapped the end of the stool with his claw like fingernails.

"Get back!" shouted Lewis.

But the Alpha could not be deterred, the pitiful humans had fallen for its trap and here it would stay. Suddenly there was an almighty thwack that brought the Big'un to its knees, for how long was anyone's guess. The Manager had taken hold of the railing once more, the very same metal railing from Primark all that time ago. Having retrieved it after his encounter with the formally living duo as a sort of trophy, a reminder of just how far he had come. Plus, it was just the right size to secure the door handles.

"Sorry sir, you don't appear to have a reservation!" said The Manager in a cool if somewhat overly rehearsed tone.

Now it was Lewis who looked at The Manager like he was a superhero, as he rained down a second blow. The Alpha was stunned and down to one knee, it turned to face The Manager only to be dealt another blow square between the eyes. Normally this would have been enough to kill a regular zombie, but this one was far from regular. Two years of consuming his own kind had changed it, not only mentally but also physically. Its cranium now thicker, made to withstand blows such as these. Its arms and legs rapidly evolved to reach its prey with ease, in short, it was the perfect human hunting machine.

The Manager went to strike him for a fourth time and had he connected, Lewis would have informed The Manager that the number four is meant to connect the mind, body and spirit. It also symbolizes the safety and security of home, which in this case would have been rather apt if it were to finish off this intruder. But it didn't connect, as the Alphas grotesque hand caught the metal railing mid swing. Now back to its feet, staring The Manager dead in the eye with murderous glee.

"Ours" it said again with a menacing growl.

The Alpha ripped the metal bar away from The Manager with minimum effort and raised it high, ready to deal a deadly blow of its own. It then jarred forward and let out an annoyed yelp as a bar stool exploded across its back, sending multiple, wooden shards flying. One of the larger shards, several inches in length, deeply embedded into the Alphas lower back as what was once blood splattered across every nearby surface. Even the high ceiling now displayed a series of black stains, reminiscent of a Rorschach test.

Everyone jolted backwards, away from the ooze, not wanting to get any on them, as there was no telling what diseases the Big'un carried.

Mistaking its attacker in the fray, the Alpha turned its attention once more towards Elinor who was stood across from it, pitchfork in hand and flanked by Zombie Stan and Zombie Ollie. Having freed them of their shackles, now poised and ready to strike.

"Get 'em boys" Elinor commanded.

Zombie Stan and Zombie Ollie lunged at the intruder, this time launching a successful coordinated attack. Zombie Stan went high, while Zombie Ollie went low, driving the wooden shard deeper into the Alpha's back. It let out a demonic sounding howl the likes of which had never been heard before. The three of them scuffling, clumsily fighting back and forth across the reception, knocking over tables and smashing chairs in the process. Luckily, there weren't any lit candles at this time of day otherwise the whole hotel might have gone up in flames.

The Manager removed the deadbolts and opened the front doors, making sure the coast was clear from any gatherings or other

Big'uns. Then retreating to a safe distance alongside Lewis and Elinor as Zombie Stan and Zombie Ollie had the Alpha pinned down. The undead duo frantically tore at the Alpha, ripping chunks of scaley flesh and thin brittle hair from its body. Scattering the discarded chunks across the tiled floor with a splat, rancid pus seeping into the grooves.

The undead duo had the upper hand and were about to finish off the job when swiftly, the Alpha twisted the wooden shard free from its own back and drove it directly into the skull of Zombie Stan.

An awful stillness filled the room as everyone watched on in horror, for a second it looked like Zombie Stan hadn't even noticed his injury as he turned to face Zombie Ollie. The two made eye contact as it sounded like he was trying to actually speak.

But whatever Zombie Stan was trying to communicate simply came out as garbled grunts as congealed blood filled his throat, blocking his windpipe. For a fleeting moment, life glimmered within his eyes once more and then, in an instant, he was gone.

"No! Please no!" The Manager cried out.

"Hey, I'm gonna get you too! Another one bites the dust" added Freddie.

Zombie Ollie seemed transfixed with what had just occurred, becoming motionless with horror, wonder, or astonishment. There was really no way to tell what was going on in that infected mind of his, but it certainly wasn't pleasant.

The Alpha took this opportunity to regather itself, its wound proving too much to continue.

"We back" it growled and fled the hotel just as quickly as it had arrived.

The attack was finally over.

Lewis was quick into action and applying the deadbolts as The Manager assisted him, fixing the metal railing back into position. The Manager then placed Zombie Ollies restrains back into place, which he allowed without fuss, still in a daze at the loss of his companion.

The Manager and Lewis surveyed the damage, as Elinor checked over Red's body, hoping for signs of life, sadly there weren't.

The attack had been sudden, devastating and deadly. The Big'un may not have accomplished its plan, but still, single handily dealt an ungodly amount of damage the residents would never recover from. The stark warning of a return swirled within the Managers frayed mind and by the sounds of it, the Alpha would not be alone.

The residents were now down to thirteen.

Stripes And The Bodyguard

Darren and Red had been affectionately known throughout the hotel as Stripes and the Bodyguard. These nicknames were coined by Avril when she saw just how well Darren protected Red on a supply run. The two of them often paired off when it came to supply runs, scouring the surrounding area for goodies. Red always sporting her signature red and black striped hoodie, somewhat reminiscent of a Freddy Krueger cosplay and Darren in his trademark black ensemble.

They worked incredibly well together, making them the go to residents for supply runs. In fact, Darren trusted Red so much, that despite the possibility of mockery he shared his irrational fear of being watched by various fowl. Admittedly she found it a bit odd, but in a world where the dead didn't stay dead and infected birds terrorised the skies, it wasn't all that strange in comparison.

Red was small and agile meaning she had been able to fit into places Darren simply could not, whereas Darren would use brute force to gain access to places that Red would otherwise be unable to reach on her own. Often swapping duties with the other residents to be paired up on these runs, something The Manager had objected to at first. But over time came to see the dynamic was most successful and was more than happy to reap the benefits.

Together they had completed hundreds of runs, but all good things must come to an end in the apocalypse, especially when it involves Big'uns. On what would turn out to be their final supply run, Red and Darren had set their sights on a home bargains store, towards the north end of the town centre. In its heyday the store had stocked plenty of dried and tinned foods, not to mention a variety of items such as gardening equipment, basic medicines, tools and toys.

The town centre had plenty of overhead cover, acting as a barrier against any infected bird attacks, which Darren and Red had seen several of in their time. The pair noticed bird attacks seemed to happen less frequently the closer to a gathering they got, which they used to safely navigate the area. Gatherings and infected birds seemed to repel each other, like opposite ends of a magnet, not wanting to share the same hunting grounds.

Red and Darren had been systematic in their approach, going shop by shop, marking each one they looted with a big red X on the front windows. This approach whilst efficient would prove to be their downfall as they had attracted the attention of the cunning Alpha. The Alpha would forgo sleeping during the day, to study the two of them as they searched the town centre, oblivious to the trap that awaited them.

Red and Darren had dealt with quite a few members of the undead community, as Red would lure them in with her speed, whilst Darren would finish them off as quickly and humanely as possible.

Of course, they never told The Manager about killing the dead ones just in case he would berate them for killing potential hotel employees.

As the two approached Home Bargains, it was clear the lack of maintenance had taken its toll. The windows had been reduced to glass splinters, the doors buckled and the entrance way resembled the film set of Jumanji. But that was part and parcel of the job these days as they carefully entered the shop, with the intention of finding some toys for the newest arrivals.

Together they quickly scoured the shop, mindful to remain silent and keep within eyeshot of each other. The air was thick and dirty, as spores of black mould hung in the air. There were droppings from all manner of creepy crawlies on the shelves, just being there made them feel like they needed a good wash.

And yet Red remained her usual upbeat self as they went aisle by aisle, taking only what they needed. "Toothpaste, yes, shampoo, yes, bath bombs, no, Red hair dye, yes!" Red whispered to herself as she went merrily about her way.

Darren was more of the quiet type but had gotten used to Red's quirky attributes.

Some of the shelving had toppled over to one side, spilling a variety of out-of-date cereal boxes across the floor, most of which had been gnawed by rats. The two momentarily split up as Darren went into the staff only area and Red disappeared towards the back of the shop where they kept the toys. They were fairly confident no gatherings lurked inside the small shop.

There were none of the usual tell-tale signs, bloody smears around door frames, bile and excrement in the corners, decaying remains, all the pleasant stuff that came along with the end of the world.

However, Darren spotted something most peculiar in one of the old offices, an old-fashioned rope snare trap. It was crude to say the very least, but still looked effective, should an unsuspecting critter scurry past. Unusually though the choice of bait was a dented and gooey looking tin of Branston's baked beans.

Darren approached the trap, puzzled as to why someone would use this as lure and chuckled to himself "what sort of idiot would fall for such a trap." When he was suddenly struck from behind, by a blunt instrument wielding figure. What sort of idiot indeed.

Hearing the commotion Red stopped what she was doing and ran to see if Darren was alright, but it quickly became apparent he was not. Darren lay face down on the ground, it was unclear whether he was unconscious or dead, either way, he needed her help. Red gently tapped his shoulders, trying to wake him, but even alerting him to the presence of a sinister looking duck couldn't rouse him.

She immediately checked to see if he were breathing, but couldn't tell if the last of the air was leaving his lungs or if his breathing was incredibly shallow.

Fully aware, she wouldn't be able to lift Darren alone, she decided the best option was to run for help. If she hurried, she could be back at the hotel within ten minutes providing nothing nasty leapt out at her. Red hated the thought of leaving her friend behind, but knew it was the best course of action.

"Hang on Darren, I'm going to get help, just stay put okay, I won't be long I promise!"

With a hop over the tangled mess that was the entrance she set off at an urgent pace.

But just outside the entrance, Red fell victim to the same assailant, as she was viciously struck on the back of the head with great force. Collapsing to the cold ground with an awful thump. Drifting in and out of consciousness as for a moment, she dreamt of being back home with Avril. Back in their cosy one-bedroom flat in Camden town, once known as the Jewel of London which suited the trendy pair quite nicely.

"Avril, come keep me warm" Red muttered as she lay, shivering on the cold pavement, blood pooling around her when she heard a familiar voice.

"That's a nasty cut you got there kiddo, reminds me of raspberry-ripple sauce." Red slipped into a deep sleep, oddly craving an ice cream covered in yummy sauce, topped off with a chocolate flake.

The assailant had followed Darren and Red, keeping a close eye from the shadows. Like Margery and blind Hank before them, their parts would prove useful to keep gatherings at bay.

No one would miss them too much the assailant reasoned. Out of the shadows stepped Hank-Two-Hands, displaying a callous smirk, disgustingly proud of himself.

Unaware though, the watcher was being watched himself, as the ever-vigilant eyes of the Alpha had seen every terrible moment. Even in its decaying mind, it wondered how a human gathering could turn on each other so easily. After all it was the Alpha's duty to protect its gathering, working for the greater good of the collective.

As it watched on, the Alpha took a step forward, accidently kicking a discarded glass bottle, sending it skittling across the pavement. The chinking sound echoed all around, as Hank-Two-Hands instantly looked up, his head on a swivel, knowing he wasn't alone. His eyes scanned every rooftop, every corner, every shop entrance, every possible hiding place. But was unable to see the Alpha, who had recoiled back into the darkest of shadows.

The Alpha watched on as the attacker quickly fled the scene of the crime. This is where the Alpha's twisted mind concocted a rather fiendish plan.

"Take the little human, ring the bell."

It may not have been the most detailed plan, but for a Big'un it was structurally sound. It waited until the other human was out of sight and leapt down from his perch, cracking the pavement on impact. Its thick, tree trunk like legs withstanding the brunt. It resisted the powerful urge to feed then and there, choosing to walk past the potential meals and collect a dust sheet from the DIY section, draping it over itself like a cloak.

The dust sheet was thick with dirt and muck, discoloured with urine stains as this particular dust sheet had been home to a nest of large rats.

Stepping over Darren's prone body, it mentally took note of where he lay, the gathering would tuck into this one later. The Alpha began to convulse, followed by a gagging, retching sound as greeny, black vomit and bile made its way up from the pit of its bloated belly, past its decaying lips and onto the floor. Walking up and down the shop, leaving its disgusting trail, like a demonic snail. The Alpha had marked its territory, as a warning to any other zombies who caught Darren's scent.

This meal was spoken for!

Then began the task of carrying Red's lifeless body as if she were a mere puppet to gain entry to the hotel. Red groaned, mumbled soft, inaudible words but remained unconscious, which was probably for the best, as they made their way back.

So came to an end the ballad of Stripes and the Bodyguard. One left face down in a discount retail chain, surrounded by a rancid mess and the other ghoulishly used as nothing more than a key, only to be tossed aside once she had served her use.

As for Hank-Two-Hands, the Alpha was indebted to him... for now.

Lockdown

Death is a funny concept, especially in a world where it's no longer permanent, but it's something the residents must face every single day. That didn't detract from the sadness that filled the hotel, Red was gone and at such a young age, Darren was missing, presumed dead and vitally challenged Stan was finally at peace.

After a thorough sweep of the hotel to ensure the other residents were all safe and accounted for. The Manager decreed that the hotel was now on lockdown until further notice.

During the sweep it became apparent that both Margery and Blind Hank were nowhere to be found. Their belongings were still safe and sound in their rooms, which indicated the worst-case scenario.

The Manager called a town meeting for the remaining residents and tasked Lewis with informing Alec, who stubbornly sat in his corrugated castle. With just thirteen people left in the hotel, Lewis tried to cheer up the boys by telling them, in Chinese culture the number thirteen is considered lucky, which suffice to say did not work. Failing to put even a hint of a smile on either Tom or Martin's bruised face, Lewis left the boys in the capable two hands of Hank and made his way back to the rooftop garden.

As expected, Alec was sitting in a worn armchair, sipping contently from his mystery flask.

"The Manager said we are on lockdown, that means the garden too I'm afraid." Lewis put a little extra base in his voice, hoping to sound authoritative, which didn't work at all.

Alec looked straight through Lewis and took another sip from his flask. "Spose you think you're in charge now then?"

There wasn't any time to appease the King of the allotments, Lewis knew he had to carry out The Manager's orders before there was another attack. Suddenly he felt very exposed on the roof, despite being several stories up, and under protective netting.

"Come on Alec, please, it's for your own safety."

"My own safety? The bloody cheek of it, my own safety indeed! Never heard such nonsense in all my life, my own safety. Bloody lockdown. Who does he think he is aye, bloody Prime Minister or something."

Lewis thought The Manager was being reasonable given the current situation, but Alec couldn't be reasoned with at the best of times.

"Yes, that's what I said, so please come down from here until we can figure out what to do next."

There was an uncomfortable silence that seemed to stretch on and on, then Alec made a vile, snorting sound followed up by a big gob of spit, into a bin beside him, that twanged like an old western film.

"Them meetings in that bloody conference room, they love all that rubbish. Makes them all feel important, when it's me up here doing all the hard graft, feeding the lot of them. Besides my back is killing me alright!"

"Backstreet's back, alright." Lewis sang off key in an attempt to lighten the mood but failed miserably as Alec just looked at him like he was mad. Obviously, pop music from the nineties wasn't his thing. Lewis was fast running out of patience, simply not having time for an old man's antics. Then he remembered Alec's Achilles heel.

"Fine, suit yourself" Lewis said with a semi smug grin. "I'm sure Elinor will understand."

Alec suddenly looked rather sheepish, no longer comfortable to maintain eye contact.

"Why exactly?" he questioned. "Say something did she?"

Lewis shrugged his shoulders. "The Manager asked her to come up here and get you herself. But I did the gentlemanly thing and offered to do it. No problem though, I will fetch her."

Alec's demeanour changed to that of a child who been given a stern telling off. It struck Lewis as odd, this power that Elinor held over Alec. Perhaps it was feminine charm, or that Alec was just of an older generation, one that didn't know how to deal with independent women. Either way the mere mention of Elinor's name seemed to do the trick quite nicely.

"Be down in five then I spose."

"Thank you Alec, I will keep a seat free for you" said Lewis as he turned away and headed through the fire exit, feeling pretty good about his little victory.

Alec surveyed his kingdom, wondering just who would look after the crops in his absence. He placed his tools to one side and tided up some foul-smelling waste buckets, not that he noticed the smell anymore. If Matt Damon could grow potatoes in his own excrement on Mars, then the king of the allotments could manage it on a hotel rooftop on Earth. Changing from his wellington boots into some scruffy trainers, Alec headed for the fire exit, taking one last look around.

He paused, suddenly overcome with a sickening sense of dread, like something was watching him. This wasn't the first time he had this feeling, often late at night he could feel piercing eyes following his every movement. Not that he told the other residents, what was the point? They all thought he was just some irritable old man, making things up.

"What good would it have done anyway" he thought to himself. "Well perhaps they would all still be alive for starters?" That was the real reason he didn't want to go to the meeting, not out of stubbornness, but out of guilt.

Between him and The Manager they knew something was out there, watching them. Each evening The Manager would come up to the rooftop at sunset, with a little something extra to top up his flask and borrow his high-powered binoculars. They knew something like this would happen one day and now he was going to have to go down there and listen to The Manager plead ignorance.

And to make matters worse, Alec knew that The Manager would probably give some sort of eulogy for his beloved Stan.

He shook off the feeling of dread long enough to realise he was putting off the inevitable, sooner or later he would have to face Elinor. He would have to admit to the one person he respected most that he knew about the Big'uns and yet said nothing.

That he may as well have killed Darren and Red himself.

For now Alec would let The Manager have his say, but he couldn't bite his tongue much longer. People needed to know the truth, that's the very least Darren and Red deserved.

"Soon" he uttered, "soon."

Alec

It is a little-known fact that the month of May is zombie awareness month, taking place mainly in America and Canada. During this month people would wear grey ribbons to signify the shadows that lurk in the light of day, whatever that was supposed to mean. People would use this as an opportunity to do some good by hosting charitable events such as zombie runs, zombie walks and zombie food drives, ironically called "Feed the dead." Unfortunately, this coincided with the actual zombie uprising that spread rapidly across the globe thanks to Mr Kingsley's virus.

Americans of all people should have been considered the most prepared nation in the world for an undead pandemic, after all their government actually had a plan for this event.

CONPLAN 8888 also known as Counter-Zombie Dominance was a U.S. Department of Defence Strategic Command document that described a plan for defending against zombies. However, the one thing this rather detailed document had not considered, was zombie awareness month. As the universe's idea of a twisted joke, people were already dressed for a part they would play permanently.

All the major news channels tried to warn the population, but this was deemed to be "fake news" and nothing more than an elaborate hoax just like COVID or Australians. By the time the penny finally dropped, it was all far too late.

With the Americans taken out of the equation, rather surprisingly the most prepared man on the planet did not own a variety of assault weapons, nor did he have any interest in the twenty-seven constitutional amendments.

This man was a simple gardener in the small town of Stevenage, called Alec.

Alec was well and truly the king of the allotments, having worn that crown since 1978. Having seen all types come and go over the past several decades, having a talent for spotting the wannabe gardeners from the real deals. The type who were mostly retired and could dedicate the remainder of their lives to growing prize winning marrow and constructing corrugated castles worthy of his throne.

What people didn't know about Alec, was that he was far more complex than his grumpy exterior would ever allow them to know. Having taken ownership of a small allotment in 1978, in which the contents of his crudely constructed but sturdy shed were an old armchair, a gas-powered barbecue, a vast collection of tools and a few bottles of cheap single malt whisky.

Most of his fellow allotment owners knew the contents of his shed, nothing to write home about. But only a very select few knew there was more to the small plot than met the eye.

In 1979 Alec ran into financial difficulty after being made redundant, coincidently around the same time Margaret Thatcher had been elected prime minister, soon finding himself on the brink of bankruptcy.

Allotment site fees back in 1979 cost three English pounds for the entire year and even in the modern age it would only cost a mere twenty-five pounds. Unfortunately, over the course of a year he had been reduced to sleeping rough at the allotment, which Alec ended up doing for over forty years. Although the majority of those years could have hardly been considered rough.

After trying in vain for several months to get re-homed by the local council, Alec decided the only person he could rely upon, was himself. With that in mind he set about a little project to correct his situation.

One day Alec decided to dig the ground upon which his castle sat, in doing so he realised that the ground was soft from years of being turned over by the previous owners.

In fact, after just a day of digging away, Alec had unearthed four feet of soil that measured eight by eight feet. In the weeks that followed he continued to dig a substantial amount of earth single-handily, slowly emptying the contents evenly onto the surrounding plots.

Using a ladder and a makeshift pulley system, not too dissimilar from the one he would help Hank-Two-Hands construct for The Manager many years later, he had single handily excavated a hole eleven foot deep.

Ever cautious, his progress was kept from prying eyes by placing dark green tarpaulin over his shed, just in case anyone got any ideas about reporting his antics. The next stage of his plan involved bringing in bricks and mortar which were easily sourced from a construction site around the corner. Under the cover of darkness, Alec took all he physically could, wheelbarrow by wheelbarrow.

This was noticed by the site foreman, who dubbed the mystery thief as "the brick ninja" a nick name Alec thought was pretty groovy as the kids would say. The site foreman had been severely chastised for losing several hundred bricks, a fair amount of timber, copper piping and precisely forty-nine bags of concrete mix.

After multiple trips and thanks to the communal watering hose, combined with an infinite amount of patience, Alec had managed to build himself an underground living accommodation.

Meticulous in his labour, Alec laid the foundation of his new home. Section by section, cement was poured, followed by bricks, insulation and plaster creating four robust walls. It may have been on the small side, but it was a liveable hole in the ground.

Towards the completion of Alec's project, his fellow gardeners naturally became curious as to what he was doing behind those plastic sheets. Considering themselves to be quite the homegrown detectives, as well as members of the national bee-keeping alliance. Two senior gentlemen immediately jumped to the conclusion that Alec must have been burying dead bodies back there and decided to investigate.

But a half-asleep Alec overheard these bizarre and false allegations, deciding it was time to put the final touches on his new home that very evening.

The next morning the two senior gentlemen returned with the pretence of watering their crops, but really, they wanted to see if there was any truth to the rumours they had created. But to their amazement the plastic sheets were gone for the first time in weeks, the shed open for all to see, Alec proudly sat inside. Filthy, covered in mud and cement, with thick, sore hands, sipping from his trademark flask, with a grin of self-satisfaction etched on his face.

The two men exchanged insincere pleasantries with Alec, as he invited them over to see how his crops were doing. Moving in closer to confirm their suspicions, the gentlemen were confronted with the sight of an ordinary looking makeshift shed.

Tools hung from hooks, various potted plants bloomed and bore luscious looking fruits. The two men furrowed their brows in confusion, trying to work out what all the secrecy had been about. But what they failed to notice was that the communal water supply had been split, diverting a secondary pipe directly into Alec's new abode. They also failed to notice a large plastic pipe in the corner of the shed that fed through the ground, into a wood stove, acting as a chimney.

Lastly, they failed to notice the old armchair, when leant back exposed a trapdoor complete with hanging ladder for easy access. Disgruntled but not wanting to show any frustration, the two men walked away, muttering to themselves about their failed theory.

Alec lived in his self-made home beyond the events of Black Sunday, living off the land above. At night he saw by gas light, kept warm by his well-insulated walls and hydrated by free water, mixed with the odd tipple of whiskey.

Alec had been self-isolating and social distancing long before the rest of the world, not knowing in a few decades everyone would be in the same boat. Throughout the eighties and nineties, he told only four other people about his home, those also being fellow dedicated gardeners that he felt that he could truly trust.

But four months after Black Sunday came to pass, Alec was exiled by one of the four he had mistakenly trusted. Who could blame them, it was the ideal hiding spot, a literal hole in the ground.

This man cast Alec out of his home whilst quoting the famous line from the 1932 film The Western Code.

"This town ain't big enough for the both of us and I'm going to give you twenty-four hours to get out. If I see you in the allotment by this time tomorrow, it's you or me!"

Alec didn't hang around for the twenty-four hours, deciding it best to make a hasty retreat, not wanting to come to blows with the well-armed man. Now considerably older and more vulnerable he wandered the ravaged streets of Stevenage, with nothing more than a rucksack of clothes and some fresh fruits and vegetables to his name. The day grew long as Alec looked for safety, trying his best to avoid gatherings and rancid birds, when he saw a strange road sign.

"Welcome to Stevenage, Home to the best hotel this side of the apocalypse, the Holiday Inn Express, ask for The Manager."

With nothing to lose, Alec decided to head to the hotel and meet this Manager person. Along the way, he managed to evade a gathering by jumping into a rubbish skip and even dodged a particularly aggressive flock of infected birds by using a dustbin lid as a shield. He arrived at the hotel, filthy and covered in foul smelling bird bile, still wielding his dustbin lid come shield, looking like Captain America had fallen on hard times.

It was here he met The Manager for the first time and after some odd pleasantries Alec bartered for food and board. In return for his skills and knowledge of growing crops as payment. Something The Manager was more than happy to accept.

Now Alec resides at the hotel, mostly dividing his time between his room and the rooftop garden, but this time he would be smart about it. Squirreling things away in case he was exiled once more, not enough to warrant any unwanted attention though.

A tin here, a few bottles of water there, clean clothes, that sort of thing. As far as he was concerned, there was only one person in this broken world he could trust, and it wasn't a grown man playing hotel.

You had to lookout for number one these days and the last time he checked, a King carried more weight than a manager.

For he was Alec, King of the allotments.

Long Live The king

"Firstly, I would like to thank you all for joining me this afternoon" said The Manager, using his best prime minister voice. "I fully understand the seriousness of the situation and would like to reassure everyone here that we will take every precaution possible to prevent any further loss of life."

Everyone was sat spaced out across the town hall, also known as conference room three with sombre expressions.

Lewis sat between Tom and Martin, an arm around each of them, having run over to the classroom as soon as the attack came to its grizzly end.

Thankfully, Hank-Two-Hands was keeping guard outside the classroom door, having heard the commotion himself. Lewis was so grateful for him keeping the boys safe in his absence, it was rare to find someone so selfless these days. But Hank-Two-Hands really was one of the good guy's Lewis thought.

The Patterson's were sat up front alongside the Darlings, eager to please as usual.

Elinor had taken place next to an inconsolable Avril. It had been her unenviable job to thoroughly check Red over for any bite wounds, oddly though there were none, the beast had simply killed Red and cast her to one side once she had served her purpose. This was of little comfort to Avril, but a much welcome relief to Elinor who wouldn't have to drive something sharp into Red's brain to prevent her coming back to life with a severe case of the munchies.

Alec stood himself at the back of the room, away from everyone else, he was only really there to show his face anyway.

Zombie Ollie had been re-muzzled and placed back into the safety of his room by The Manager himself, although he couldn't help but notice how docile he was, as if he too were in mourning.

"Zombies don't really have feelings, do they?" he thought despite his well-known stance on how the formally living should be treated with dignity and respect. It never really occurred to him that they had thoughts and feelings of their own, but perhaps there really was a glimmer of humanity lurking beneath all that rotting flesh.

Conspicuous by their absence were Margery and Blind Hank, both of whom had vanished without a trace. At least this was the story according to Hank-Two-Hands.

Lastly but by no means least, Hank-Two-Hands had taken up a seat next to The Manager at a long white desk, facing inwards towards the residents. He was wearing fresh, clean clothes after Mr Darling pointed out his left sleeve had something red all down it, presuming it to be Red's blood from the Big'un attack.

Mr Darling was right, it was indeed Red's blood, just not from the attack.

Apart from the occasional sobbing sounds from Avril, the room remained totally silent, which made The Manager incredibly anxious. This sort of thing wasn't in his job description, but the hotel needed some damage control, that much was clear. When he took on the mantel of The Manager, he imagined every room occupied, expanding his empire outwards, creating a proper chain of hotels.

People would have come from far and wide just for the privilege to stay, bringing with them a plethora of rewards to show their gratitude. But now his numbers were dwindling and people were looking towards him for a plan of action.

"I ... I erm, what I mean to say is" he stuttered, unconsciously bouncing his left leg underneath the desk.

"What The Manager means to say is that until further notice we are to remain in total lockdown" Hank-Two-Hands quickly chimed in, to which The Manager gave him a nod of approval.

"So, outside is now off limits, that includes the rooftop and there won't be any moaning about it!"

There was an audible murmur, they hadn't been on lockdown before, but it didn't sound like much fun. The murmur quickly escalated into a dull roar, like walking into a Weatherspoon's pub on a Friday night, pre–Black Sunday of course.

Hank-Two-Hands banged his fist on the table, which quickly silenced everyone once more.

"As I was saying, the rooftop is now off limits, so we gotta bring everything down and place it in reception. The crops should grow just fine, once that's all done, we can have a funeral on the roof before locking up tight."

"You can't just go messing about with them crops, the plants will die if not done right" Alec huffed.

"Then it's a good job we have you to show us how it's done isn't it, Alec!" shouted The Manager. No one dared make eye contact with one another.

"It's just us now and I intend to keep it that way, we can't lose anyone else, I won't allow it. Darren, Red, Hank who happened to be blind, Margery and Stan. All people who should be here in this room with us right now, but they aren't." The Manager's voice was low and soft, trailing off.

Avril stood up and ran out of the room sobbing uncontrollably as Elinor glared a hole straight through The Manager.

"She might still be alive if you opened up the door sooner, maybe that thing would have gotten spooked or something. I don't know, maybe it would have thought twice if we all opened up together, but you had to prove your stupid point didn't you." Elinor shouted, trying unsuccessfully to hold back the tears and then ran after Avril.

The Manager fully understood her frustration wasn't really directed at him, at least that's what he hoped. Sometimes it was all just a bit too much being in charge, but it came with the territory, besides, it wasn't without its perks. Hank-Two-Hands gave The Manager a firm nudge from underneath the table, snapping him back into reality.

"Eh-hem, yes well, I understand emotions are high and..."

"It spoke!" Interrupted Lewis.

"I'm sorry what was that?"

"I said it spoke, it said ours and then it said, something about coming back!" Everyone in the room turned to face Lewis.

"Is no one here going to address the fact, that thing could bloody well speak!"

Everyone then turned their attention back to The Manager to gauge his reaction.

"Erm, maybe the kids shouldn't be present for this bit? Hank-Two-Hands suggested. "You alright if I take these two rascals next

115

door, think I saw a portable DVD player in the classroom and a copy of Shrek Two."

Even if Lewis had wanted the boys to stay, they were already off their chairs, climbing past him to join Hank-Two-Hands. He simply couldn't compete with the allure of an actual film, hell even he would rather watch Shrek two than be here.

"Thank you, Mr Two hands, that is very much appreciated." said The Manager.

"Hey just call me Hank yeah? Seems silly the whole Two Hands thing, now the other one is gone and all."

No one was actually sure if the other Hank who happened to be blind was dead or just missing, for all they knew he could have trapped himself in a wardrobe somewhere, but it was very unlikely.

In any case to suggest he was "gone and all" seemed rather callous on Hank-Two-Hand's part.

"Erm, I suppose that makes sense, Thank you Hank, that's very kind of you." There was an air of doubt in The Managers voice as he wondered if this was the right time and place to bring that topic up.

But would there ever be a right time for such things The Manager thought to himself.

The now "just Hank" gave a nod, accompanied with a slight grin and stood up from his seat, making his way out of the room. Stopping briefly as he passed Alec, the two exchanging sideways glances.

"I'm onto your games mate" Alec whispered as Hank's grin turned into a big toothy smile.

"No games here, matey, just a story about an ogre and his donkey." Hank shoulder-barged Alec as he passed, making sure no one else in the room caught sight of the satisfied look on his face.

Alec just shook his head, wondering if things would have been better had he stood his ground, staying at the Allotment.

But the ever-increasing ash cloud had blocked off the air pipe to the underground abode, suffocating the new inhabitant in his sleep.

"As you were saying Lewis" The Manager prompted.

"That thing, that beast could speak." Lewis reiterated. "Now I don't know about you lot, but in my experience, they aren't usually too chatty! Not only that, but it actually set a trap for us, it wanted us to open the front doors!"

"I mean come on, that thing didn't even bite Red, as it probably didn't want to risk her turning midway through its plan! That's what we're dealing with here."

The was an audible gasp followed by whispering voices.

"Will it come back darling?"

"I hope not darling, that thing sounds positively maleficent "added the Darlings rather unhelpfully.

The Patterson's, Mr and Mrs each took turns speaking, but it all sounded as if someone was speaking with a mouth full of toffee, so it was just met with polite smiles of acknowledgement before swiftly moving on.

"Lewis, I'm not sure what you thought you saw or heard, but please let me reassure everyone in this room that zombies." The Manager caught his slip of the tongue and quickly corrected himself. "Excuse me, the living impaired are incapable of speech. Believe me poor Stan never uttered a single word in all his time with us."

The Patterson's and the Darlings nodded in agreement.

"After all, we cannot even be certain that was a formally living person, now can we? Interesting fact, a family of people with blue skin lived in Kentucky USA for many generations. They were called the Fulgates of Troublesome Creek and are thought to have gained their blue skin through a combination of inbreeding and a rare genetic condition known as meth, meth, METH-EMOG-LOBIN-EMIA." It took a few attempts to pronounce, but The Manager was able to spit the complicated word out.

"Perhaps this is a similar case?"

"Hah!" snorted Alec. "I bloody-well told him that fact!"

Lewis looked towards Alec as they both exchanged a series of looks, silently telling each other to discuss things in private at the appropriate time. The meeting was not going the way The Manager wanted as he desperately tried to get things back on track.

"In any case if you would all please proceed to the rooftop and help remove the crops. They are to be replanted at the back of

117

reception, once done we will have a funeral service before we go into lockdown. Meeting adjourned!"

"But, what about?"

"I said meeting adjourned." The Manager slammed his fist on the table, so hard it sounded as if it would splinter into a million pieces. Obviously, Lewis wasn't going to win this battle, despite the truth of the matter. He couldn't understand why it was being covered up like this. If the Hulk T-shirt wearing beast made good on its word to return with reinforcements, then all the bar stools in the world wouldn't be enough to fend them off next time.

The Darlings and the Patterson's quickly got up and left the room, keen to avoid the crossfire of any further arguments. As far as they were concerned, lockdown was a good thing, if they never had to go outside ever again, then so be it.

The Manager walked over to Lewis who stood up to confront him. "You and Alec are to oversee the garden move; you have two hours." Before Lewis even had a chance to respond The Manager proceeded to briskly exit the room and lock himself into conference room four, to which only he and Hank had the keys.

"*I say, oh no, no no, I say, oh no, no no, I fight authority, authority always wins, I fight authority, authority always wins.*" 1983's Authority song by John Mellencamp began to play, so loud that it made the walls vibrate, in a blatant disregard of house rule number four.

Lewis was seething, angrier than he had ever felt in the last two years, it was all well and good for The Manager to lie to himself, but to the other residents? This was something that he could not stand for.

"Pick your battles" said Alec who was still standing at the back of the room.

"But he."

"Listen, know when to concede yeah? Now help me lug all the garden stuff down, the bloody Darlings won't be any use!"

Lewis conceded for the time being as prompted, thinking that carrying out The Manager's orders would put him into a more approachable mood.

He quickly checked in with Hank and the boys who were all sat on the floor watching Shrek two on a small nine-inch screen. A film that former prime minister David Cameron had once referred to as "cinematic genius" a statement that both Martin and Tom would probably agree with.

Lewis left them to it, as the last thing he wanted was to cause the boys anymore upset.

The next two hours were filled with a variety of expletives as raised plant beds were emptied and moved from point A to point B.

The Patterson's Mr and Mrs were tasked with getting the heavier items downstairs, as quite frankly they were both the broadest now Darren was gone.

The Darlings oversaw replanting everything at the other end while Alec and Lewis took everything apart top side. Both Elinor and Avril had been excused from duty for the time being, even if The Manager did want them both to help. Keep calm and carry on and all that business, not that he would dare to say that to them right now.

It just wasn't worth the argument.

The reception area was quickly transformed into a makeshift greenhouse, the overturned tables and blood splattered walls also cleaned up. Something the Darlings weren't too keen to do, but were left with little choice. Only the original silver conduits and extractor fans were left behind on the rooftop as everything else was stripped bare. Alec even kindly offered to tear down his beloved corrugated castle.

"You can use the wood from my shed if you want, you know for the girl" he said to Lewis, who wondered what he meant exactly. But Alec clarified his intentions by miming fire.

Out of all the recent casualties and disappearances, only Red and Zombie Stan could be put to rest properly, as for Darren, Hank and Margery they would have a memorial plaque made in their honour.

"The Manager will want to do the same for Zombie Stan, you know that right? asked Lewis.

Alec rolled his eyes but knew he was right. "We better get on it then hadn't we."

They tore down the shed, neatly piling up the wood, making sure to leave enough room for two bodies. Neither of them were experts when it came to cremation but figured it should be enough kindling to do a decent job.

Satisfied they had done all they could, Lewis and Alec set about the unenviable task of collecting Red and Zombie Stan's bodies, which had been covered up with bedsheets and placed into one of the empty rooms on the ground floor.

It didn't take long for the pristine white sheets to become stained with an array of disgusting colours, reds, blacks, browns and greeny-yellows seeped through, making a horrid, sticky mess. Both Alec and Lewis wore thick gardening gloves, not wanting to touch the rancid rainbow of bodily fluids, and respectfully as possible, began the arduous task of carrying Red's body up the stairwell.

"It really did speak you know" said Lewis, whilst carrying Red's upper half.

"What did?" asked Alec.

"That, thing. I've never seen anything like it, but on my boys' lives, I swear it spoke actual words."

Alec remained silent apart from the occasional straining sound, he was older than he cared to admit and as light as Red was, carrying her was still physically demanding.

"I guess you don't believe me then?, Elinor was there too, she will back me up, just ask her!"

Alec stopped in his tracks, they were only halfway to the rooftop and he could have done with conserving his breath.

"Big'un was it?"

Lewis nodded.

"Sort of wearing a torn up, dirty old gym shirt, with one of them superhero things on it?"

"How'd you know that?"

Alec started to walk forwards again, prompting Lewis to keep walking backwards.

"Big'uns, that's what we call them, that one you saw is their leader from what I understand. Keeps them all in line and fed."

Lewis wanted to stop but, with Alec pushing onwards, left him with no choice but to keep going. "You mean to tell me you knew about it?"

"Mm-hmm" Alec confirmed. "Couple of others know about them too, but it's all hush hush."

"Well what else do you know; how many are there? tell me!"

"I know that you oughta mind where you're walking."

Lewis was suddenly pressed up against the fire exit to the roof top, as he angled his elbow to push the bar down and with a well place back kick the door flew open with a bang. They staggered over to the pile of kindling and gently laid Red down.

"Easy, she ain't a sack of spuds you know!"

"I'm being gentle Alec!" Lewis said frustratedly. Just a week ago he had been camping and now he was lugging bodies around. This wasn't what he had imagined life at the hotel would be like at all.

"So, as you were saying?"

"It's not my place to tell you, that's for The Manager, but" Alec trailed off.

"But what? Please I have kids here, you have to tell me."

Alec walked over to the edge of the roof and looked down to the ground below, no longer keen to keep eye contact with Lewis.

"You get to see all sorts from up here, people practically forget you even exist. Out of sight, out of mind as the old saying goes. All I can tell you is that those things, they ain't the real monsters. They're just hungry is all, doing what comes natural to them now."

Alec paused and took a deep breath. "I'm not in a good place Lewis, not mentally I mean, but just stuck in this bloody hotel for god knows how long. You know things are bad when you miss living in a hole in the ground."

Lewis approached Alec and contemplated placing a hand on his shoulder, but held off. Where was Elinor when he needed her, she would know just what to say, after all she was like the daughter Alec couldn't marry off.

"Get them kids out of ere, that's the best thing you can do now." As if on cue a cold wind picked up and swirled around them, Lewis half expected a clap of thunder followed by some chilling organ music.

"Give me a hand with that Stan thing and we can talk about the rest later, yeah?"

Lewis wanted answers then and there, but knew the more he pushed Alec the more withdrawn he would become. Still, it wasn't a very reassuring discussion, especially the comment about Tom and Martin. But for now, Lewis would have to show some restraint and simply nodded towards Alec, as the two made one more trip back down the stairwell to collect Zombie Stan.

The smell was a horrid mixture of rancid, decaying, and putrid flesh, barely masked beneath the vile stained bedsheet. Every time they moved him, spores of dead skin and pus became airborne as both of them struggled to hold their breath. The stench brought tears to their eyes, as neither of them dared utter a word for fear the aroma would land on their taste buds.

It seemed to take double the amount of effort, but finally they made it back to the rooftop. This time however, they weren't so careful with Stan's body as they hoisted him onto the kindling with a clumsy thump.

"It's a shame we couldn't call housekeeping to do that for us" said Lewis in a vain attempt to lighten the mood, but Alec just stared blankly into the distance, like he had already mentally checked out.

"Did you know that dance fever was this month-long plague in Strasbourg France, odd thing that was. Bloody hundreds of people went and danced for about a month for no apparent reason, they actually danced themselves to death."

Alec began randomly spouting facts off, like he had done so many times before. Only this time he was lost in a thousand-yard stare, after taking several big gulps from his flask. Lewis looked at him in irreverent silence, unable to quite understand the point Alec was trying to make.

"So, when you think about it, maybe all of this ain't so strange now is it, people think of new ways to kill themselves all the time. Just this time it's a bit more bitey."

"Right?, well I had better get the others then, it's getting dark. We can talk later this evening though, yeah?" Said Lewis awkwardly.

He wanted to ask Alec if he was alright, even though the answer was clearly no. They were both, stressed out and tired but knew there was more gardening to be done. Calling it gardening made carrying bodies around a little easier to deal with mentally.

Lewis silently backed away, leaving Alec alone with his thoughts and headed towards the fire exit, with the weighty metal door slamming shut behind him. Alec had always been big on respect and Lewis had earned his today.

In the space of a single day Lewis had seen off a Big'un, stood up to The Manager, helped move the crops, and most importantly given Red a final farewell.

Alec took another swig from his flask, only for it to produce a morsel of fluid. "Typical."

He walked over to Red, whose body was still covered from head to toe in the stained sheet. He always had a soft spot for the girls here. Admittedly it had taken him a while to get used to the idea of two girls being in a relationship, but that was just the way he was brought up.

Boys were meant to be with girls and girls were meant to be with boys. Back in his day anything else was labelled as seedy and usually belonged within the confines of the top shelf of a magazine shop. But the world had moved on from such archaic ideologies and reluctantly, so did Alec.

Holding up his flask, He peered into the small spout, confirming it was indeed empty. Respectfully as possible he placed it next to Red, making sure to tuck it under some kindling. Alec had been a resident of the Hotel long enough to know there was only one way to check out, and it didn't involve walking out the front doors.

He had seen too many people suffer the same fate as Red all thanks to The Manager and what he considered to be his convoluted ideas.

Not to mention Hank, he never did trust that man, always sneaking around, lurking in the Managers shadow.

Alec snapped out of his thoughts long enough to realise that the rest of the residents would be joining him shortly, to send off their fallen friend and the previously living Stan. He occupied himself in the meantime by placing any remaining bits of wood onto the pile, when it occurred to him, they hadn't taken down the protective netting above.

If the flames reached high enough then the whole thing would light up the night sky like a firework display, enough for every walking corpse within a ten-mile radius to see.

He should have waited for Lewis to return, but instead opted to deal with it himself before the others arrived. Taking a pair of scissors from a toolbox stashed inside an old extractor fan, he planned to cut directly above the cremation area. Draping the netting around the kindling at a safe distance.

Once done he could then simply cable tie it all back together, at least that was the plan.

Alec reached up whilst on his tippy toes, stretching out his fingertips as far as they would possibly go, but the netting was still a good foot out of reach. There was no way around it, he would have to stand on the kindling, choosing to perch himself on Stan's side, rather than disrespect Red.

"Scuse me mate, just be a minute" he said while gently pulling himself onto the wobbly platform.

Reaching up, the netting was now within reach, as he made sure to take a good look around for any possible nasties. It looked to be all clear, but Alec had failed to notice a flock of decaying pigeons circling the skies directly above, watching his every movement.

He began to cut into the netting, one link at a time, carefully ensuring not to cut more than needed when suddenly a gust of wind swept past him. He stopped, taking another good look around, inspecting the surrounding edges of the opposite buildings, there was nothing as far as he could tell.

Sadly, Alec's vision was not what it used to be, thanks to a combination of age and living underground, he was practically more mole than man.

Had he managed to get to Specsavers more often then perhaps he would have seen a formally brilliant pigeon swooping down towards him at great speed.

The infected birds' soft coos now replaced with a more formidable screech, launching a full-scale assault on its prey, just managing to slip through the freshly cut gap.

Alarmed, Alec managed to get his hands up to protect his face but fell backwards, directly on to Stan's corpse as something sharp dug into his leg.

"Argh, get off me you sod!"

Funnily enough, the winged beast didn't take much notice of Alec's pleas and continued its assault as man and formally living fowl, clumsily fought in an epic battle of good versus evil. Alec tried his best to get back to his feet, when suddenly, four more long dead pigeons joined the scuffle, incensed by the smell of fresh blood. Luckily for Alec the others were not so coordinated, having even worse eyesight than him, as they became tangled up in the netting.

But the first undead pest still had the advantage, as it pecked and clawed at Alec with sheer ferocity. That was until Alec fell off the pile of kindling, falling flat onto his front, crushing the bird with a sickening crack. Jumping back to his feet, he attempted to close the hole before the others got in, but the birds were flailing around too much to secure it properly.

Alec grabbed the dangling piece of netting and quickly cable tied it back into place, as best he could, having to hop up and down to reach, whilst avoiding getting his fingers pecked. Every hop sent a lightning strike of pain down his leg, feeling like walking over flaming charcoal with a three-inch rusty nail in his heel!

"Bloody vermin, nearly got me didn't ya, eh."

He said, puffing for breath as adrenaline pulsed through his protruding veins. Then he saw it, a rotten pigeon claw embedded in his right leg.

"Well, ain't that just a kick in the teeth."

The claw was twisted and misshapen, more resembling a dried dog treat than anything from a once graceful pigeon. It had snapped off just above his knee, as Alec gave it a light tap, causing him to wince in pain. A hot sensation shot throughout his entire body, but the area was ice cold to touch.

There was no doubt about it, he was infected.

"Well, dancing to death suddenly don't seem all that bad" he muttered, knowing his fate was sealed.

There was still a gap in the netting where Alec had hastily put it back together, not massive but still big enough for one of the birds to get inside if given the chance.

He left the mangled claw protruding from his leg, collected several cable ties from his toolbox, then climbed back onto the pile of kindling.

"Argh!" Alec cried out in pain as the claw caught a rogue piece of wood, causing him to slip and land directly onto Zombie Stan.

"Sorry bout that mate, not as steady on my feet as I used to be."

Zombie Stan's lower jaw came clean off, falling in between the slats, which would cause untold distress for The Manager. It took a moment for Alec to steady himself atop of the platform as he slipped his fingers through the netting. In an instant the other decayed pigeons began to peck at him, drawing even more blood. Ignoring the pain, Alec repaired the hole, link by link. Ensuring his final act would be to make it safe for the other residents.

The birds were ravenous, managing to rip flesh from bone liked winged piranha, but Alec couldn't be deterred as finally the hole was repaired.

"Sorry lads, I'm off the menu I'm afraid."

He stepped down and dusted himself off. This wasn't how he imagined going out, but all things considered, he had taken pride in making a difference at the hotel. Each day the residents had gone to bed with full bellies, content in the knowledge there would be food on the table the next day, all thanks to him.

Alec had imparted enough knowledge onto Elinor to keep things running smoothly in his absence, just another thing he could take pride in.

He took a notepad and pen from his toolbox, dusted off a spot on the ledge and sat down as the sun began to set in the distance. From here he could see most of Stevenage bathed in the warm glow of sunlight and for a moment all the troubles of the world, simply washed away.

Even the decayed pigeons seemed content with their fresh strips of finger meat, and fluttered away to settle in for the evening. Alec wiped his hands down the length of his jumper, smearing blood across the dark green wool. His wounds looked awful and stung like hell, but he wouldn't let that be the focus of his final moments.

He began to write a letter for the next ten minutes or so, occasionally stopping to watch the sun disappear beyond the horizon. The once white paper now a mixture of smeared ink and blood, intended to be read at a later date.

Alec then tore off a piece of paper, neatly folded it and placed it back into his toolbox, safe in the knowledge that it was just a matter of time before the others found it.

"Oh well, that's that. At least she will be alright, that Lewis bloke will look after her. He seems alright I spose."

Alec had been a survivor his entire life, preferring to outlive his enemies. But a man must admit when he's beat, and this time, he was well and truly beat.

Gently lifting the netting, he gingerly climbed onto the ledge.

"Long live the king."

Alec then took a deep breath, closed his eyes and stepped forward.

The residents were now down to twelve.

Conference Room Four

Before Alec made a terrible mess of the pavement, The Manager slammed the doors to conference room four shut with an almighty bang. It was so loud it could be heard two floors up. He secured the doors and proceeded to crank up the volume on his portable music player, drowning out all the worries of the outside world.

"Uh it spoke, didn't you hear it" he said aloud in a mocking tone.

"Uh, I think you're mistaken; it did speak actually."

"Bloody Lewis, uh I want to speak to The Manager. Honestly, we should start calling him Karen! Both him and that Alec, nothing but trouble the pair of them."

The Manager slumped into an old office chair and slowly spun himself around, as was the traditional thing to do when it came to office chairs. The mysterious conference room had always been off limits as stated in rule number five and with good reason. Most assumed it was a place where The Manager and Hank produced their various contraptions to stave of the ever-approaching dead.

The Patterson's once tried to sneak a peek inside, but the doors were fortified with a clunky metal chain, threaded through the handles and topped off with a heavy-duty padlock.

They thought about removing the handles with a screwdriver, but the clanking of the metal chain echoed down the long, empty hallway. They quickly concluded it wasn't worth the risk, as whatever was inside couldn't possibly be as valuable as a roof over their heads.

But how wrong they were, as conference room four was filled from floor to ceiling with pre-packaged food, medical supplies, clothing, tools, toys, games, just about anything you could possibly imagine. The Manager had acquired his cave of wonders by discreetly taking half of Darren and Red's supply runs over an extended period of time.

To him, conference room four was his own personal Lonely Mountain, Erebor, the greatest city in Middle earth, filled with untold riches and he was the mighty Smaug.

This room didn't just hold materialistic treasures though, as hidden in the far corner of the room were two doors. Past the leaning tower of marshmallows, door number one was a secret exit, leading to a car park that was more jungle than concrete these days.

Well-hidden behind tall grass and weeds, this was The Manager's own personal means of escape should things go sideways. In fact, the entrance was so well hidden that neither Darren nor Red had spotted it during their many supply runs.

Door number two led directly to Zombie Stan and Zombie Ollie's room. Well just Zombie Ollie's now. it imperative these two doors were never mixed up.

The Manager liked to keep his undead companions close by, offering them some warm-blooded company every now and again. In his mind, it was important to mingle with them to a point they could be domesticated. It hadn't been easy, but over time The Manager had formed a rapport, to the point they only tried to bite him on the odd occasion. Which any zombie enthusiast would tell you is real progress.

The Manager continued to slowly spin in his chair, replaying the events of the meeting in his mind as he listened to Zombie Ollie clumsily shuffling behind the second door.

"No gratitude, that's the problem."

He gave the wall a stiff kick, which sent a tidal wave of chocolate bars directly into his lap like the Fonz and his classic jukebox trick. The Manager put all the ill-gotten chocolate back into the box, keeping one aside for himself, removing the wrapper and shoving it into his mouth all at once.

"Bloody Lewis" he said although it was hardly understandable, with a mouthful of gooey caramel chocolate.

Usually, conference room four would offer The Manager much needed solace. It was his inner sanctum in which he could plan out operations, expand his empire or just stuff his face until he felt sick. But he was starting to wonder if running a hotel was worth all the stress, especially now he had everything he could possibly want.

Enough food to last him several years if rationed properly, plenty of classic eighty's music and a reception full of crops. He contemplated sending the entire group of residents on a supply run and promptly changing the locks once they were all gone.

"I could turn the lights off and pretend not to be home. That would show the lot of them."

But the reality was he needed them far more than they needed him, as The Manager preferred to delegate rather than get his own hands dirty.

The main door handles began to rattle, giving The Manager a fright as the familiar sounds of Hank's keys jangled, echoing down the corridor. The Manager hastily finished his chocolate and hid the evidence In his breast pocket as Hank entered.

"Oh sorry, didn't know you was in here boss, just setting about me rounds for the day."

The Manager quickly stood up, turning his back and wiping his mouth to hide any evidence.

"You're telling me you didn't hear the music?"

Hank chose to ignore the wall shaking eighties music marathon, simply shrugging in a display of ignorance.

"Oh, forget it, is there something you want?"

"I just need to make sure the door to Ollie's room is locked tight. He was all riled up and there's no telling what he might do if given the chance. For all we know them two are the reason Hank who couldn't see and Margery went missing."

That comment didn't strike The Manager as true, but still it wasn't worth the risk. He gave Hank a dismissive nod and sat back down, once again slowly spinning around in his chair.

As Hank passed through, he felt a tug at the back of his jacket as if to gain his attention.

"Help you with something boss?" he said, turning to face The Manager who stopped spinning.

"No thanks Hank, just do what you need to do."

Hank gave a returning nod and set off, when again he felt yet another tug at the back of his jacket.

"Yes boss, what is it?"

The Manager just looked at him with a puzzled expression. "I literally just said, do what you need to do?"

"Oh, right, it's just that, um."

"Sometimes I feel I've got to, run away I've got to, get away." 1981's tainted love by Soft Cell began to play, drowning Hank out.

"Well never mind, I will just go sort Ollie out."

Hank made it as far as the door this time before he felt a third tug on the back of his Jacket. This time however he turned around to the sight of a certain ghostly boy hiding behind The Managers chair.

"I give you all a boy could give you, take my tears and that's not nearly all."

Hank tried to speak but the ghostly boy raised a single finger to his lips, instructing him to remain silent. Hank always did as he was told when it came to his kids, wanting nothing more in the world than to keep them happy and safe.

"Zombie Ollie says he's really bored and wants to come out and play" said the apparition. "He's all alone and misses his friend."

Hank slowly nodded in agreement. "Must be lonely, losing Stan and all."

The Manager looked up, wondering why Hank was still hanging around.

"Erm, yeah I suppose so, the place does seem a lot emptier without him."

The Manager may have well been speaking as clearly as the Patterson's, as his words failed to reach Hanks ears. The ghostly boy however had Hanks undivided attention.

"Let him out now, take him to the roof to say goodbye to Zombie Stan, it's only fair."

There was a long awkward pause that filled the room like a giant balloon.

"Get away, you don't really want any more from me, to make things right, you need someone to hold you tight" the lead singer of Soft Cell added, helping to break the silence.

In the blink of an eye the boy was gone, which didn't resonate as the slightest bit odd, in Hanks fragile mind.

"Right, then, spose I'm off to do what I need to do."

The Manager gave another dismissive nod towards Hank, who finally left the room, taking the awkward feeling along with him.

Equipped with a new set of instructions, Hank would be sure to carry them out to the best of his ability. As second in command at the hotel, it was his sworn duty to keep the lights on and the guests happy.

And what could possibly make everyone happier than including the formally living Ollie to say goodbye to his companion. Perhaps serving as a much-needed morale boost, giving him a new purpose in life.

Something to really raise his spirits.

Something to really sink his teeth into.

Another One Bites The Dust

Hank cautiously entered Zombie Ollie's room which was virtually pitch black, apart from a slither of light piercing through the boarded-up windows. The once royal blue carpet, now black, sticking to the soles of his shoes with every step sounding like tearing Velcro.

Hank felt around for a lantern just past the doorframe and attempted to light it. There was a thick tar like substance coating the handle which smelt awful. He used his jacket to wipe off the goop and lit the burner with an old plastic lighter he kept on his person.

The light erupted in the darkness, forcing the shadows into exile, ironically momentarily blinding Hank. As his vision returned Zombie Ollie was suddenly mere inches from his face.

Zombie Ollie had silently glided over to Hank across the pus ridden floor, like a hellish ice skater. His sunken, rotten, mustard yellow eyes, fixed firmly on Hank.

"Blimey, don't do that Ollie, you'll give me a heart attack if you ain't careful."

Zombie Ollie didn't even flinch, he just stood there unnervingly, his hands still bound together and mouth gagged shut.

"You miss your mate dontcha? Must be lonely being in here all alone."

There was a quiet sadness about Zombie Ollie, like a piece of him was missing and not just the bits that had fallen off. He looked lost, even afraid, who knew what was going on in that infected mind of his. It was uncertain if any human thoughts remained, rattling around like The Manager had insisted. Or if he was just a savage beast that just wanted to feast.

"Let's get you to the roof yeah? Say goodbye properly." Hank took Zombie Ollie by the arm, attempting to lead him out of the room, but he was less than forthcoming.

"Come on fella, you know me, don't be playing games, we ain't got the time to muck about."

But Zombie Ollie remained steadfast, his eyes piercing a hole through Hanks delicious looking head. Even he could sense there was something rotten about Hank, and it wasn't just the gunk covering his jacket.

"Ah, I know what you want, you want your hands free dontcha, that's fine by me fella" Hank said as if placating a child.

He reached into his trouser pocket which seemed to contain an infinite number of useful items and took out a small red, retractable knife. Zombie Ollies hands had been crudely but effectively bound together with duct tape, so tightly that chunks of dead skin were peeling off at the edges. Hank proceeded to gently glide the blade through the tape in a satisfying, perfectly straight line until his hands were free.

Zombie Ollie looked down at his now free hands and began to stretch his fingers out wide, allowing the congealed blood to slop through his protruding veins.

Hank watched in amazement as the formally living man before him casually shook the pins and needles sensation from his extremities. But what came next was truly extraordinary.

Now with the feeling back in his hands, Zombie Ollie gestured for Hank to hand him the knife, complete with a muffled grunt. Unsure if he was seeing things, Hank stood there in revered silence. Again, Zombie Ollie gestured towards the knife.

Against his better judgement, Hank complied with the undead one's request. Retracting the blade, handing it over, which Zombie Ollie was all too keen to accept.

It took a few attempts to extend the blade, as Zombie Ollie's fingernails were brittle, his thumbnail falling off altogether with a sickening squelch. But finally the blade was exposed.

He then lifted the knife to his face and began to slice through the muzzle. It had been a good while since Zombie Ollie used such a tool, as he accidently sliced deep into his own face. Damn near taking out one of his eyes numerous times.

But his perseverance was impressive, and soon the muzzle fell to the floor, freeing his blackened chompers. Then just as casually, Zombie Ollie retracted the blade and handed the knife back over to Hank who stood there in awe.

The formally living man then stretched out his jaw, as if chewing on an Everlasting Gobstopper and grunted.

"Grrrr, ooo" almost like he was trying to speak.

Hank was flabbergasted, keeping his eyes fixed on his companion.

"Don't mention it fella, so you good to go?"

Zombie Ollie grunted once again and looked as if he may be trying to nod his head. Was it possible? Was the Manager right all along? Could the undead really be rehabilitated? Hank had never really bought into the idea, but he couldn't pass up a roof over his head for a few quirky ideologies.

But stood before him was living, or in this case formally living proof.

Perhaps there were others like Zombie Ollie out there, trying their best to regain their lives. But that would have to be a discussion for another time, due to the more pressing matter of the funeral.

"Come on then, let's get you up to the roof, that will be nice wont it" Hank said, addressing Zombie Ollie like a toddler.

Hank took hold of Zombie Ollies arm and attempted to pull him along, but this brought on a sudden change of temperament. He began to growl, like a dog backed into a corner, baring his teeth, warning Hank off. Hank clearly didn't get the message as he held firmly on to his arm, pulling towards the door. Zombie Ollie quicky reached his tolerance, lunged forward, sinking his teeth deep into Hank's forearm.

Strangely Hank didn't yell or scream, there weren't any expletives, instead he calmly tried to prize his attackers rancid grip free.

It wasn't a pleasant sight as several of Zombie Ollies teeth broke free of his rotten gums, embedding themselves deep into Hank's flesh.

There was a revolting, sloppy tearing sound as skin ripped and tendons tore away.

"Come on now fella, that's not very nice, let go now."

But there wasn't any deterring Zombie Ollie, if there was a man in there somewhere, he had been shoved aside for the wild, feeding animal.

"Alright that's enough, don't forget whose been feeding you yeah! I kept the best bits of Margery and Blind Hank for you."

Zombie Ollie paid no notice to his meals ramblings and continued to slurp down delicious chunks of human flesh.

"Look if you don't let go, I'm gonna have to do something about it, now do as your told, last chance!"

How Hank was able to calmly deal with such excruciating pain was simply extraordinary, he remained eerily calm under the pressure of literally being eaten alive!

It was like Hank's mind had disconnected from the situation, as if he were watching it happen to someone else.

Left with no other choice, Hank flicked the blade open and slashed at his attacker's throat. Zombie Ollie finally relented, his undead eyes displaying a look of betrayal, like he couldn't believe what this human had done. But Hank couldn't give Zombie Ollie another opportunity to attack, and jammed the knife through his left eye. The impact was so great, that the blade snapped off, deep within Zombie Ollie's Brain.

Just as Zombie Stan had shown a flicker of humanity before passing on, so too did Zombie Ollie. The cloudy vail lifting from his eyes, showing a more human hazel green colour, which was actually quite beautiful.

For a fraction of a second, he was plain old Ollie once more, but just as quickly, he was gone.

Plain old Ollie slunk down to the sticky floor with a thud and a squelch, crumpling awkwardly in half. The wound to Hank's arm was simply horrendous, as blood trickled down to his fingertips. He removed his belt, using it as a tourniquet, which was rather effective in stemming the flow.

In the back of his mind, he knew he was done for, if he didn't bleed out or lose the arm to gangrene, then the virus would claim him.

Hank poked the fleshy bite mark and winched as his ghostly companions appeared in the far corner of the room, hidden in shadow, looking concerned for their dad.

"Are you okay?" asked the girl meekly.

Hank rolled his sleeve down and hid his arm behind his back.

"Me, never felt better kiddo, him on the other hand, well he's feeling a bit sleepy."

The boy and girl looked at the crumpled mess that was Zombie Ollie.

"He won't be coming with us to the funeral I'm afraid. Don't matter though, at least we will be together yeah?"

The boy and girl looked sad, emerging from the shadows, giving their father a hug. Their hands passing through him until they vanished altogether. Hank's arm began to cramp and tremor as the virus launched its attack on his immune system, but amazingly he composed himself.

He checked his greasy hair and left the room as calmly as he had entered, still keen to be on time for the funeral. But the clock was well and truly ticking.

Usually, the dead came back within ten minutes of being bitten, but the time could vary from minutes to hours if the victim still had a semblance of a pulse. In any case the funeral was shaping up to be the event of the year, that was for certain.

The residents were now down to eleven.

Isaac

Leaving a trail of congealed sticky, black blood, the Alpha retreated to the safety of its den. Unlike the hotel for the living, the gathering preferred to remain confined to just one room. They were stronger this way, a more cohesive unit, that would devour all before them like a brood of termites.

However, not wanting to show its wounds to the others, the Alpha removed itself from the gathering. Standing alone in a burnt-out room on the fourth floor, watching flickering human shadows on the rooftop across the way. Although the Alphas right eye had mostly rotted away, its left eye was able to focus on his prey with eagle like accuracy.

It yelped as a sharp pain cascaded throughout its rotten body, like a familiar sensation of a long-buried memory. The Alpha ran it's claw like, elongated fingers along a three-inch-wide scar underneath its grubby T-shirt as it recalled discomfort coming from its unnaturally bloated belly. Something had happened in the before time, something that sent the mighty Big'un crashing to the floor in pain.

The Alpha struggled to put its thoughts together, but sometimes, if it tried really hard, images would form in its infected brain.

The scar felt bumpy, protruding slightly as it continued to leisurely run its fingers back and forth across it. Images flickered in and out of its minds eye, it was difficult to stop them from fading away into the darkness, but there was one that was becoming clearer.

Men, human men were watching, trying to hurt, no wait that wasn't right. They were helping.

They were, doing something, something with sharp things, what did the humans call them? they were shiny and pointy.

"Nnn, nnnives, nives" that's it, they used nives on him, to take something out of him, something bad, something that was broken.

"App, pen, dix." it sounded out a strange word, not knowing the meaning behind it.

A complex word, but one that had great meaning for the Alpha. It closed its eyes and continued to run the tips of its fingers along the scar.

"App, pen, dix" it sounded out again, slowly. It really had hurt; in fact, this strange appendix thing had nearly killed it good and proper long before Black Sunday. But the humans in blue clothes had got it out just in time. Oddly though they had chosen not to eat it.

"What a waste of tasty human meat" it thought.

The Alpha's back wound was weeping, its blood so thick and gloopy that it helped to seal the deep cut quickly. Sometimes being a zombie had its advantages it would seem, minus the lack of a cure of course.

Unless you count Haitian folklore, in which it is said to free a zombie of its undead state, its best to either feed them salt or lead them to the ocean. The zombie will then become self-aware and attempt to return to the grave. But as the closest ocean was a little over sixty-eight miles away and the restaurant downstairs was closed, salt really wasn't an option for the Alpha.

It sat down with a cloddish thump, crushing an old bedside cabinet in the process, and looked out the window to the overcast skies above. There was a calming stillness in the air this evening, which helped to sooth the Alpha.

That was until the stillness was broken by a sound far off in the distance.

It was a sort of whooshing sound, similar to swinging a thin stick quickly through the air. But as the sound grew closer, it changed to a horrid scraping noise, like rusty nails on a chalkboard. There isn't much that makes the Alpha nervous these days, but whatever this thing was, certainly put it on edge.

It squinted its one good eye and peered out of the smashed window, the thick jagged glass littering the once immaculate carpet. There was something out there, something flying around, much bigger than the usual infected birds that dotted the night sky.

The Alpha sat and watched in awe as a winged creature came into view, it was rather majestic in a terrifying, able to rip your face off kind of way.

The winged thing glided towards the shattered window, seemingly on a direct path for the Alpha, closing in fast. The Alpha stood up with a pained grunt, it's back still causing discomfort as it took hold of a splintered table leg.

Poised and ready to knock whatever was approaching clean out of the air like a grim cricket player, with any luck it would go down easily and taste delicious.

But the winged thing looked off kilter, becoming more contorted, struggling to fly straight. One of its wings was nothing but bone as it frantically flapped the other. Trying to balance itself out, struggling to lift its top-heavy body. Lunging through the window, with a flurry, it landed surprisingly well onto an overgrown plant, trying to gain its bearings.

The room fell silent as the two locked eyes.

Puzzled, the Alpha wasn't sure what to make of it all, other than it hadn't decided to attack, at least for the moment.

The winged thing slowly opened its intimidating beak and let out a screech, a truly terrible sound, like dropping shards of metal into a blender. The Alpha covered its ears, desperate to drown out the noise, but demon bird persisted. The alpha just wanted a bit of peace and quiet, but even that was too much to ask it seemed.

Then a curious thing happened as the Alphas rancid mind translated the blood curling screech into actual words, picking out syllables and vowels amongst the noise.

"Tasty humans over there, better get a move on ain't cha" it said with a thick east London accent.

"You, talk?" The Alpha grunted.

"Too right I can, I know all sorts me. I'm what you call Isaac.

Before Black Sunday, this particular fowl was once a white-tailed eagle show bird. Taken from one county show to the next, tolerating sticky fingered children petting him, in return for a lovely fresh mouse. Amazingly his name really was Isaac, as reflected on an identity tag which the Alpha must have subconsciously seen, piecing the letters together like a jigsaw puzzle.

Alone and hungry, Isaac was in search of a new master, and the Alpha would do nicely.

"Hurt, see?" the Alpha grunted once more, pointing at its wound.

The Isaac thing stretched outs its wings, displaying an intimidating two and a half metre wingspan, even if most of it was nothing but bone.

"Get the gathering to do it, ya idiot! You tell em what to do and they do it, simple init."

The Alpha wasn't sure if the bird's advice was sound, the fight had taken a heavy toll.

"Stop touching it or it will get infected!"

"Sorry" Grunted the Alpha, quickly moving its hand away from the sticky wound. "But what if humans fight again?"

The Isaac thing screeched repeatedly like it was thoroughly amused. "They don't stand a chance, not against us!"

There was no denying with a new companion and with the human ranks at their weakest, now was as good as any time to strike. The Alpha stretched out its arm invitingly for the Isaac thing which triggered a long dormant command.

In an instant it fluttered and hopped onto the Alphas arm, graciously accepting it as his new master. Without a traditional leather glove, used to tether the eagle and protect the Alpha's arm.

The bird sank its talons straight into the Alphas flesh with an oddly satisfying squelch.

Isaac began to nibble at the intestines around the Alphas neck, feeding on the putrid organs. Clearly the two had accepted one another, each finding a new sense of confidence. The Alpha pulled its tattered gym shirt down over its wound and went downstairs to join the gathering, passing through a series of darkened winding corridors, down several flights of stairs.

Leading into a large room with two red armchairs and a coffee table, dramatically set up in front of an old fireplace. One of the Big'uns was kneeling, trying to light a fire using a disposable lighter. But the fireplace was just for show, only containing some realistic plastic logs. This Big'un was missing its thumb, and repeatedly dropped the lighter after each attempted use. Having been trying to get the fire going without success for several months now.

The Alpha entered the room cautiously, concealing its wounds, trying its best to look as strong as ever. The twenty strong gathering of Big'uns turned towards their Alpha, stupefied at the sight of the decaying Isaac thing firmly clinging onto its arm.

The Alpha gave a short, sharp grunt that was completely ignored by the gathering, so it grunted once more. An animal, almost pig like sound to make up for its inarticulate nature, but still nothing. It grunted again angrily, managing to gain a few Big'uns attention. But still a few others chose to ignore it, preferring to focus their attention on the bird.

"Hello, you adorable little nuisances." The Isaac thing screeched, which seemed to finally do the trick.

The Alpha's mind could hear the bird speaking clear as day, while the rest of the gathering could only hear it for what it really was, a decaying, hungry bird. But even so, this was enough to gain their undying attention.

"Eat them all, humans" the Alpha grunted.

These words resonated within three or four of the Big'uns infected grey matter as they understood what their Alpha was getting at. The others would be more than happy to simply follow the majority as long as they could reap the rewards.

The Alpha began to beat his chest with its one free arm, in a gorilla like show of dominance. Slowly, keeping a booming, steady war drum style beat, summoning the gathering into battle.

It didn't take much to get them all riled up, roaring with anticipation, ready to feast on fresh meat. This time there would be no stopping the Alpha, for tonight they would dine like undead royalty.

The residents of the human hotel were about to be reduced to zero.

Tom And Martin

Lewis collected the boys, who had been having the time of their lives watching a tale about an ogre and his donkey companion, blissfully unaware that Alec had gracefully stepped off the roof, and then not so gracefully landed with a splatter onto the pavement outside.

The mood was sombre, like a thick fog had filled the hallways, as the trio remained silent on the way to the rooftop. Keen to break the silence, Lewis prompted the boys to tell him about their first day of class.

"Come on you two, did you at least have fun listening to Hank's stories?"

Tom and Martin shrugged their shoulders half-heartedly.

"Well at least tell me what you learnt about today" insisted Lewis.

The boys looked at each other before producing several folded drawings from their pockets, that they created throughout the day.

"Mr Hank said he needed to go out for a bit and wanted us to draw some colourful pictures," said Tom. "To cheer the place up a bit."

This was the first instance Lewis had learnt about the boys being left unsupervised and was not impressed to say the very least.

"But he was meant to be watching over you, he promised me. What if that thing got into the room, God knows what would have happened!"

Lewis understood he had left the boys unattended multiple times in the past with nothing more than a tent to keep them safe. But that had been deep in the countryside well away from your regular Joe zombie, with the exception of the gathering that had rumbled their hiding place.

But this place was meant to be better, as the sign stated it was meant to be "The best hotel in the apocalypse."

Food, shelter and new friends had been a welcome and much needed change of pace, but it was starting to come at too high a price. Lewis wondered if this was what The Manager meant all along by "affordable prices."

"So where? Why? Where?" Three excellent questions Lewis demanded answers to. "I mean, he was guarding the door when I saw him, wasn't he?"

Not prepared for a sudden line of interrogation, the boys sheepishly averted their gaze.

"He said he needed to go out, didn't say where" answered Tom. "When he came back, he warmed up some beans for us to eat. You know, for lunch, but gave us a bit extra."

Martin nodded in agreement. "He said not to tell anyone just in case they got mad. We're really sorry."

Lewis wasn't the slightest bit angry towards the boys, he fully understood the power of hunger was more than enough to sway the most noble of men, let alone two hungry boys.

Still, he was furious with Hank for leaving them unattended for all that time, especially during the attack.

But Lewis didn't want to show his frustration, just in case the boys wouldn't be so forthcoming in the future. Instead, he would take Alec's valuable advice, knowing when to concede, but rest assured Hank was in for a battle.

Lewis abruptly stopped walking which in turn caused both Tom and Martin to stop dead in their tracks. He knelt and put his arms around them both, bringing them in for a big hug.

"Hey, I'm just glad you two are safe. After all I need you two to keep coming up with cool names like Dreadnought for me." Lewis whispering the last part, keen to avoid any eavesdropping from the others.

The boys both gave their dad big smiles, as the trio continued towards the rooftop.

"Mr Hank did tell us a joke before he left, do you wanna hear it?" asked Martin, who was eager to share.

"Go on then, let's hear it."

"Did you, no wait that's not right, why did, erm." Martin clearly needed to work on his comedic timing. "Oh yeah that's it, do you know why you should never challenge Death to a pillow fight?"

"No, why?" asked Lewis.

"Because you would have to deal with the reaper cushions."

145

Martin grinned, waiting for his dad's reaction as Lewis let out a chuckle at the awful joke.

"Ha, very good mate, you should tell it to the others. Just maybe not today" he quickly added. "You know, as it's probably not a great idea to joke about death with the funeral and all.

Emotions were running high enough without Martin doing an ill-timed stand-up routine. But given time they would pass. They might pass like a kidney stone but regardless they would pass.

The boys had never been to a real funeral, or a Viking style cremation for that matter. Their mother had died on Black Sunday while they had been in their dad's care. They held a simple farewell ceremony by lighting candles in her memory.

This was the best they could do as unfortunately Lewis was unable to locate all of her body parts. Martin was too young to comprehend the awfulness of the situation at the time, but it was always something that stuck in Tom's mind.

With just one more flight of stairs until they would reach the rooftop, they suddenly heard what sounded like a mixture of drunken laughter and sobbing coming from a utility cupboard. Lewis stopped, as did the boys and listened intently.

Muffled voices followed by raucous laughter were undoubtedly coming from the small cupboard as Lewis approached.

1984's cheesy pop classic "Like a Virgin" began to play loudly for all to hear. Somehow the occupants of the cupboard had managed to gain access to a music player of their own, as the door began to vibrate thanks to Madonna's famous lyrics. Clearly, they had taken some of The Managers cassette tapes, which certainly wouldn't go down very well. Lewis pressed his ear against the wooden door, to determine just who was inside, when he heard Elinor's distinctive voice over the music.

Hoo, like a virgin! Sang Madonna proudly.

"Don't think there's many of those around here" added Elinor as her companions all laughed hysterically before one of them belched uncontrollably. "Oops, scuse me."

Lewis turned to the boys who were both thoroughly amused and impressed by the loud belch, giggling to themselves.

"Okay, you two, I think they might have had a bit to drink by the sounds of it. I'm just gonna pop my head inside and make sure they are alright. Then we will finally get to the roof."

Both Tom and Martin nodded, standing quietly for their dad, that was until Martin's stomach made some interesting noises of its own which made them both giggle again. With all the commotion from the attack and moving the garden, Lewis hadn't spoken to Elinor all afternoon. He wanted to make sure she was okay and perhaps discuss their near kiss.

But that would prove tricky, seeing as she was sequestered away with company.

There were hundreds of spacious rooms to choose from at the hotel, but upon opening the door Lewis saw Elinor, Avril, Mrs Darling and Mrs Patterson. They were all huddled together in the small cupboard, sharing several bottles of Tesco's finest red wine.

"Darlings, this cab-er-nay-saw-vee-nyon is more delicious than I remember, said Mrs Darling as she struggled to pronounce every syllable.

Light crept in from the now adjacent door which quickly caught everyone's attention, bringing an abrupt halt to the conversation.

"Sorry for intruding ladies, I just wanted to say we are headed to the rooftop now."

There was an uncomfortable silence as Lewis brought them all back down to reality.

"Yeah, um, so."

"We will be up when we are good and ready!" snapped Avril.

There were no ill feelings on Lewis's part, as he completely understood grief does funny things to a person. Just the thought of losing the boys filled him with dread, but it was always a possibility in today's desolate world.

"Thank you Lewis, give us a few minutes and we will be there" said Elinor to cover for what could be mistaken for rudeness on Avril's part.

Lewis didn't dare utter another word and backed out of the cupboard, making sure to pull the door shut behind him. The boys had remained silent the entire time as asked, but not due to their dad's instructions. Lewis turned back towards his boys, only to be confronted by the unexpected sight of Hank, standing directly behind them. His grubby looking hands planted firmly on each of their shoulders, bringing with him a sense of unease.

"It's nice to have more kiddos in the hotel ain't it. My two were getting a bit lonely."

Puzzled as to what Hank meant, Lewis took a step forward, but quickly held off as both Tom and Martin began whimpering with pain. Hank was digging his bony fingernails into their shoulder blades, applying enough pressure to draw blood, which was starting to seep through Martin's t-shirt.

"Stop, you're hurting them!"

But Hank stood firmly in place. "You dunno what you're talking about, kids need to be tougher these days. No telling what nasty things might get a hold of them if they ain't careful."

Instinctively Lewis reached out to forcibly remove Hanks two hands, but once again, Hank applied pressure as both boys yelped with pain and began to sob. Tom tried to pull away, but like an anchor, holding a ship in place, Hank was simply too strong.

Unsure what to do Lewis kept his distance for the moment, as like a virgin came to an end, in which Madonna had concluded that it felt quite good inside apparently.

The cupboard door clicked open as the ladies of the hotel all stumbled out one by one, into the unusual scene. Hank took his hands off the boys and took a step back as an unbearable silence filled the hallway.

Elinor quickly realised the boys were upset, as tears streamed down their faces. Lewis pulled both Tom and Martin towards him in a protective papa bear manner, keeping his eyes firmly locked onto Hank.

"Stay away from my boys, you hear me! You even think of coming near them and it will be the last thing you ever do!"

The ladies of the hotel sobered up in an instant, unable to comprehend what they were seeing. Hank was the trusted second in command of the hotel, but that looked as if it were all about to change. Lewis stood tall with his best aggressive looking stance, placing the boys behind him.

"Hey, we're all friends here ain't we? We need to stick together, to keep the real monsters out."

The boys were physically shaking with fear, no doubt they would have nasty bruises from Hanks unusually firm grip. Elinor moved in to have a closer look for herself.

"Did he do this to you two?"

They both nodded in unison and cowered deeper into their dad's arms for protection.

Avril who was still dealing with Red's death, slowly began to make a discreet exit, which prompted Mrs Patterson and Mrs Darling to do the same.

"Oh, come on, them boys need toughening up, they can't even handle a little pat on the back every now and again," said Hank mockingly.

Lewis couldn't tell if he was trying to cover his tracks, or was just plain delusional, either way he was not best impressed.

"The next time I tell you to leave them alone, I won't be doing it with words."

Hank grinned wickedly with a malicious glint in his eyes. "You lot can't take a joke can ya, well that's the last time I do you any favours mate, you understand. I mean, who else you gonna get to teach them for you?"

Elinor stepped in between the two, fuelled by anger and several glasses of Sauvignon, but Lewis swiftly pulled her out of harm's way.

"Pfft, you lot honestly, I'm gonna inform The Manager about this, just see if I don't."

Hank's demeanour changed rapidly from threatening to defensive, all the while looking past Lewis and company to his ghostly companions. They stood there, mocking the boys by pulling silly faces, pretending to cry.

That's when Lewis noticed the trickle of blood running down Hank's arm. Alarmed by the sight of this, Lewis immediately inspected both Tom and Martin's shoulders.

"What else have you done? Why are you bleeding? Who else have you hurt?"

Hank suddenly looked very shaken, as all the colour drained from his face. His mind instantly went to Margery, Red, Darren and the other Hank who happened to be blind before his untimely passing.

"Dunno what you mean, I ain't done nothing."

But the truth was etched all over his grizzled face, something had happened as the trickle of blood became more apparent.

Lewis no longer had the patience for Hank's deceit as he forcibly took him by the arm, revealing a rotten toothed bite mark. It was instantly clear that something nasty had gotten a hold of Hank, and this was the reason he was acting so strangely thought Lewis.

"Hank I, I'm so sorry, how did this happen?" Lewis was suddenly racked with guilt.

Hank recoiled his arm like a toddler and rolled down his sleeve. "You'd be best to mind your own business. Like I said I ain't done nothing, now if you scuse me, there's things that need tending to."

Hank tucked his shirt in, attempting to look somewhat composed. Then walked towards the rooftop without uttering another word, leaving everyone to wonder if the hotel was as safe as The Manager claimed it to be.

Lewis and the boys had only been residents of the hotel for a short while, but their old tent was starting to look more and more appealing with each passing day.

Lewis and Elinor exchanged a series of concerned looks, but it was clear something was rotten in the hotel, and it wasn't Zombie Ollie. The two of them silently ushered the boys back downstairs, as far away from Hank as possible.

In hindsight perhaps it would have been best if Elinor had gone to the roof to warn the others.

"Hi everyone, my sincere condolences, oh by the way Hank is going to go all Dawn of the Dead at any moment" that sort of thing.

But instead, they went back to room one-oh-five, still shaken by the experience. But in the immortal words of Taylor Swift, they would have to "shake it off," as it was in this room Lewis and Elinor would hatch a plan to check out of the hotel.

It was time to tell Elinor about Dreadnought.

Dreadnought

"You have a what nought?"

"We have a car, which is called Dreadnought. But that's not really the point." Lewis walked over to the window and opened the curtains, in yet another blatant disregard of rule eight.

"It's not far from here, just around the corner, stashed in an underpass. Look I have the keys and everything."

Lewis went into the bathroom only to return with a yellow plastic duck, who was wearing a little rainbow wig.

Elinor looked at Lewis like he was stark raving mad.

"Erm dad, that's Sebastian and he's just a toy duck" said Tom stating the obvious.

"What? No, I hid the car key inside the duck, look! Lewis held up the plastic duck to the flickering light of the lantern revealing the silhouette of a key.

Elinor looked out of the window, squinting to see this "Dreadnought" but was unable to see anything of note.

"This car of yours, it runs?" she asked. "It's just that I thought petrol only lasted like, three to six months. They said it a bunch of times on the news before Black Sunday, to stop people from over stocking up the stuff."

Lewis shrugged his shoulders, "I dunno, I mean some of my spit went in there too. What does it matter if it works?"

Elinor contemplated the gravity of what Lewis was offering, the hotel clearly wasn't safe, not with the Hulk t-shirt clad brute and Hank running amuck. She wanted to tell Lewis, that she had seen that very same zombie six months ago. That she had watched it rip her boyfriend apart with ease, like pulling the wings off a daddy long legs. But with Tom and Martin in the room, decided it was best to keep that information to herself for the time being.

In any case, could she really leave everything behind for a guy she had only known for a week.

"I don't know, what about Avril, she's all alone here. Can we really just up and leave?

Lewis looked at the boys who were both still shaken from their encounter with soon to be formally living Hank.

"We can't stay, it all seemed so good at first, especially meeting you. But too much has happened, too many people are getting hurt, and with the Big'uns, well I can't see any other options. Plus, the fact that Hank is a walking time bomb."

The whole situation was rubbish, in every sense of the word, but Elinor knew Lewis was right, besides, it was always her intention to leave once the time was right.

"Can we take Avril with us? Is there room for us all?"

Lewis smiled; it was such a relief not to have to do this on his own again.

"I think we can squeeze in one more."

Elinor smiled and once again used a well-placed hair stroke "thank you so much!"

They needed to gather provisions as discreetly as possible, not only for the journey but also to set up their new home, wherever that maybe.

The general plan was to head north, hoping they would happen across a place where they could finally settle down from this nightmare, perhaps somewhere in the countryside. Maybe they could start a farm, full of fluffy bunnies and other cute animals.

Maybe they could sit under the stars each night, roasting marshmallows, that were well past their sell by date. Just maybe.

Both Tom and Martin were disappointed at the prospect of losing fresh food and soft beds, but fully understood the dangers that surrounded them. Once Avril had been informed and packed up, it would be time to check out of the hotel, permanently.

*Bang, bang, bang! * They were suddenly interrupted by distressed pleas on the other side of the door.

"Let me in quickly! let me in!"

Lewis raced to the door, as Elinor quickly sat with the boys on the sofa, placing her arms around them protectively. The door flew open to reveal a frantic and blood splattered Mrs Darling. Accompanied by a visibly shaken Avril, her face completely drained of colour.

"What happened? Are you alright?" asked Lewis.

"Do I bloody look alright to you? No, I'm pretty far from alright" said Mrs Darling, letting her false posh accent slip. "You have to do something, its Hank, he's gone bloody mad!

"He killed my husband!"

The Funeral

Lewis and company were conspicuous by their absence as only seven of the residents had turned out for the funeral. The Darlings, the Patterson's, Avril, Hank and The Manager had all gathered around for the hastily put together cremation.

The Manager hated Funerals, or any public event for that matter, due to an old family superstition. Three of his family members were said to have died at public events, with the cause of death ranging from simply falling over to being impaled on a garden rake. Hence why he ensured all garden tools would be safely tucked away in the reception area.

"Is this everyone?" Asked the Manager. "No Elinor, no Alec, or Lewis and the boys?"

No one verbally answered, opting instead to shrug their shoulders in response, except for Hank who coughed and retched.

"Urgh, scuse me, something must have gone down the wrong pipe." Hank was starting to look rather worse for wear, but to the unsuspecting residents this was seen as a mixture of stress and chilly weather.

"I'm guessing that Lewis and Elinor are off somewhere playing happy families. As for Alec, well he'd rather throw himself off the roof than lose his precious garden" said Hank, not knowing just how right he was.

"Sod the lot of them, they ain't got no respect."

Hank then began to cough violently, hocking up big clumps of dark green phlegm, as everyone took an immediate step backwards in disgust.

"Perhaps we should just be getting on with it yeah?"

The Manager thought about patting Hank on the back, but decided against it, as there was no telling what illness he might be carrying. The Manager looked overhead, and took note of the netting that still covered the roof.

Thinking it was odd that Alec had left it up, but knew there must have been a good reason. It didn't matter too much though, he reasoned to himself. As there was more than enough spare netting at the back of conference room four to repair any damage the fire might cause.

Everyone stood in a semi-circle unsure of what to say, clearly it was up to The Manager to get proceedings underway.

"Well firstly, thank you all for coming, it would have meant a lot to both Stan and Red, I'm sure."

There was a symphony of sobbing from Avril, and spluttering from Hank, cutting off The Manager mid-sentence.

"Right well, um, perhaps some music and then we shall commence."

The Manager had brought along his beloved music player, which in the grand scheme of things probably wasn't the best idea. Not only were they about to light a beacon for all to see, but also pump out some tunes just for good measure.

Avril, bleary eyed from a combination of red wine and crying, perked up with the mere mention of music. Red and herself loved nothing more to sing their favourite punk rock songs of the early noughties when they were together.

"Oh, that would be nice, do you have The Black Parade by My Chemical Romance at all?" that was Red's favourite song."

The Manager didn't know what a Chemical Romance was, or a why they would have a parade, let alone a black one.

"Erm sorry I'm afraid not, but I do have something that I feel fully encapsulates Stan's essence. Oh and Red's too."

Avril muttered a few choice expletives under her breath, before being drowned out by Tina Turner's hit, "The Best." Which was actually one of The Manager's more recent songs amidst his collection.

"*I call you when I need you, my heart's on fire, You come to me, come to me wild and wired, Oh, you come to me, give me everything I need.*" Tina sung loud and proud for all to hear as Hank clumsily fumbled with the plastic lighter at the base of the kindling.

No one had really taken into consideration just how damp and ash sodden the rooftop had been.

In the movies, someone would fire a flaming arrow from a considerable distance, hitting their chosen target with impressive accuracy. Leading to an instant inferno and a rather beautiful send off as they floated gently across a still lake. But between the coughing and spluttering, Hank was having a difficult time getting the fire going.

"Bloody thing, can someone run downstairs and get some oil? Otherwise, we will be here all sodding day!" As far as funeral services go, this was one of the less heartfelt affairs.

"Um, Hank is that really necessary? I mean wouldn't that be rather disrespectful" asked The Manager.

Hank hocked up something black and horrible smelling, as it splattered against his shoes.

"They're dead if you didn't notice, some more so than others. Now let's hurry this up, I've got a pounding headache."

The residents huddled to one side, held in unison by an uncomfortable quietude. Mrs Darling placed her arm around Avril, whispering something to her, which didn't sit too well with Hank. "

You got something to say? Hmmm? How's about less yapping and more fetching." Hank spluttered, again bringing up more of the black tar like substance.

"If you must know, I was telling the poor girl to ignore you. I must say Hank, you are being quite rude" said Mrs Darling as her husband nodded in agreement.

The effects of the virus were really beginning to take their toll, as Hank's vision and hearing, rapidly became impaired. Not to mention a noticeable hunger, deep within the pit of his stomach, that was getting difficult to ignore. But despite the debilitating venom coursing through his veins, Hank's sense of smell vastly improved at a remarkable rate.

"Shame you don't look as good as you smell."

"Hank are you feeling alright?" asked The Manager.

"Yeah, never better, why you asking for?"

"You don't look too well Daddy" said the girl apparition, abruptly appearing alongside her brother, standing just behind The Manager.

"Yeah, you should eat something" added the boy, pointing towards the residents.

Dazed and out of sorts, Hank threw the plastic lighter towards the netting at the edge of the roof. But it managed to sail straight through, falling to the ground below with a clatter.

The Manager threw his arms up in frustration, and tutted in typical British fashion. Hank didn't take notice though as the venom had seeped into his cerebral cortex, chipping away at the final pieces of his mind.

"You really should lock that door; we wouldn't want anyone sneaking off" suggested the ghoulish girl.

"Cheers Kiddo, hadn't thought of that."

The Manager looked at Hank with a befuddled expression. "Sorry, who exactly are you calling Kiddo?"

Hank didn't answer, now fully immersed in his own little zombie world. A world where the living were second class citizens and the dead were the ones in charge.

Hank took hold of his comically large bunch of keys and fumbled for the correct one, finding it in record time. On auto pilot he proceeded to push past The Manager, and locked the exit with a resonating clunk.

"Now just see here, what on earth do you think you are doing!"

Hank's response was far from what The Manager expected, as he inhaled a deep whiff of his scent, allowing his primal instincts to kick in.

"Too gamey, not good enough. Need something proper meaty."

Now the ghostly apparitions stood either side of Mr Darling. "This one looks tasty" said the boy.

"Yeah start with him" added the girl.

Hank proceeded towards him and rolled up his sleeves, revealing the dirty black chomp which caused a collective gasp.

"Hank who did this to you?" asked The Manager. "We can help you, just please stop whatever it is your planning."

But the scent of Mr Darling's inferior vena cava, pumping blood to his juicy vital organs was just too appealing to ignore. Like a shot, Hank lunged at Mr Darling with bloodlust in his eyes, sinking his teeth deep into his neck. There was a blood curling scream, followed by a sickening gurgling sound as Mr Darling gasped for breath. Mrs

Darling ran for her life, leaving her husband in the clutches of a now blood-soaked Hank who was tearing into him like a juicy Christmas ham.

"Please somebody, do something!" she cried out and cowered behind The Manager.

The Patterson's being the burliest leapt into action, trying their best to pull Hank away. But even they struggled with his vice like grip, as he continued to rip chunks from Mr Darling who wailed horribly. The Patterson's rained multiple blows down to no avail.

Hank's eyes rolled back into his head like a feeding shark, caught in a frenzy.

Blood splattered across the rooftop at an alarming rate, soaking both Hank and Mr Darling like a scene from Carrie. Even if the Patterson's were able to pull him away, the chances of saving Mr Darling were slim to none at this point. The Patterson's shouted and screamed in their muddled accents, whatever they were saying couldn't have been suitable for young ears.

"Awa' n bile yer heid ya Boggin Dobber!" bellowed Mr Patterson.

But Hank was unusually strong, seemingly getting stronger the more he fed, tearing through Mr Darlings neck like a possessed chainsaw. Both Avril and Mrs Darling cowered behind The Manager, away from the gruesome sight when suddenly there was a series of booming thuds from behind them. Turning to face the source of the sound, someone, or thing was on the other side of the fire exit, practically shaking it off its hinges.

Thud, thud, thud! Resonated as flesh angrily met steel.

The Manager looked towards the flailing mess that was Hank and Mr Darling, realising he still had the keys on his person.

Thud, thud, thud! Once more the door shook violently.

Whatever was on the other side wanted to get through in the worst possible way, but no one dared risk getting the keys.

Thud, thud, thud! This time louder, more violent, indicating the return of the Big'un, seizing the opportunity to attack.

This was enough to momentarily gain Hank's attention, allowing the Patterson's to launch him clear across the rooftop, and drag what was left of Mr Darling away.

Thud, thud, thud! The thick metal door bent slightly outwards.

Anything that could have been used as a weapon, had been neatly placed downstairs in the reception area, leaving the residents completely defenceless.

The Manager kept Mrs Darling and Avril behind him protectively, whilst simultaneously trying to stop Mr Darling from bleeding out. But his wounds were too severe., there were chunks missing from his neck, face and forearms, right down to the bone. Even if he were to survive past today, Mr Darling would succumb to the virus.

The Patterson's looked to be faring better, now having the upper hand against the wild beast that formally was Hank, laying into him with stiff kicks and punches.

Thud the door moved again, this time splitting the surrounding wooden doorframe.

Thud the door finally gave way, revealing the hulking figure of a blood splattered and heavily bruised furious monster.

It was Darren.

"I don't suppose anyone has seen that bastard Hank at all?"

Everyone's jaw was agape, as in unison the residents pointed towards the entangled mess that was Hank and the Patterson's. Darren didn't hesitate, flying into action, ripping a chunky, damp piece of kindling from the stack with complete disregard for the bodies that lay atop. He meant no disrespect untoward his fallen friend. Darren simply had tunnel vision, zoned entirely on Hank.

"Bet you didn't expect to see me again so soon huh!" Darren yelled as he viciously swung the kindling directly at Hanks head, just for him to move at the last moment, and catch Mr Patterson square in the face.

Mr Patterson collapsed into a motionless heap with a repulsive thud, blood trickling from his hairline. This gave Hank a much-needed reprieve as he was now back on his feet, snarling with insatiable hunger. He was at an odd stage of the transformation, somewhere between living and dead, as the last of his neurons fired, commanding him to take control of the hotel by any means necessary.

Darren swung once again, this time connecting with Hank's right arm, but it had no effect. The wood snapped clean in two, clattering across the rooftop in an explosion of splinters and ash. One of the pieces ricocheted straight into The Managers portable music player, sending shards of grey plastic in every direction.

"Baby, I would rather be dead" Tina Turner stated as she was abruptly cut off.

"Feckless, the lot of ya." Hank said with a scowl. "I made this place what it is, and" more rancid bile spewed up, deep from within Hank's bowels cutting him off midsentence.

Bumbling backwards, Hank fell into Alec's old toolbox, spilling the contents with a clatter. There were a variety of items, pruners, assorted wire, screws, but most notable a bloody, smeared piece of paper. Caught in the breeze, skittering across the rooftop towards Avril.

She looked at the neatly folded, yet stained note and picked it up. She didn't know why, but something told her it was important.

She placed the note into her back trouser pocket just as Mrs Darling and The Manager escorted her through the now open fire exit. Leaving Darren and the Patterson's to deal with Hank. Mrs Darling didn't want to leave her husband behind, but knew there was nothing more that could be done. By taking him, they were risking their own lives even further.

Mr Patterson wiped the fresh blood from his brow and nodded towards Darren, welcoming him back into the fold. The three of them each taking another piece of kindling, this time Darren noticing Red's body. This only served to enrage him even further as he lunged at Hank without any consideration for his own wellbeing.

"You killed her, why, why'd you do it you monster!?"

Darren connected several stiff blows across Hank's arm and shoulder as the Patterson's tried to assist but were unable to get a clean shot amongst the fray.

"Got to fill up the buckets with something don't I."

Hank spewed the contents of his stomach across the rooftop, catching and temporally blinding Darren like a Dilophosaurus.

"You lot didn't seem to mind what was in the buckets, as long as it kept the gatherings away."

Darren fell to the floor, wiping chunks of Hank's innards from his eyes as the Patterson's just stood there, in shock.

"Urgh! I can't see, someone grab him!" Darren called out.

But Hank was even faster than anticipated, leaping onto Mrs Patterson, sinking his teeth into her shoulder, with such force that he tore straight through her thick coat. Mrs Patterson yelped and screamed horribly but was unable to fend off her attacker. An irate Mr Patterson, clubbed and battered at Hank, but was taken down with a single swipe.

Still blinded, Darren stumbled back to his feet, relying on his hearing alone to determine where his foe was. With burning red eyes and arms outstretched, he blindly felt his way towards the awful sound of Mrs Patterson being eaten alive. Clumsily falling flat on his face with an "oof."

Darren continued to wipe the gunk from his eyes, and was finally able to see, but his vision was terribly blurred.

Hank managed to pull himself away from the delicious Mrs Patterson and taunted her husband, begging him to come to her rescue.

"What's in your head? In your head? Zombie, zombie, zombie-ie-ie-ie, ha-ha" said Hank with a malicious glee, as he launched yet another full-on assault towards the Scotsman.

Who knew Hank was such a big a fan of the Irish pop band, The Cranberries.

Instinctively Mr Patterson held his arms out to protect his face and neck, but Hank wasn't a fussy eater and happily tore two fingers free from his hand.

Tendons and exposed bone dangled as blood gushed in all directions. The sheer volume of gore on display would have made the heartiest of men recoil in horror. Mr Patterson knew what being bitten meant and slumped down next to his wife who lay in an ever-growing pool of her own blood, gasping for life.

Oddly, Hank stepped back to a safe distance, looking at the wonderful mess that he had made.

"Plenty of meat to fill them buckets with now, The Manager will be pleased."

Darren crawled over and sat with the Patterson's, all the while keeping a blurred, yet vigilant eye on Hank. "You don't know what you're saying. If that were true, then how come you left me and Red to die in that shop?

Hank smiled a perfectly evil smile. Several of his teeth now dislodged, protruding from his cheek. How there was any humanity left in that rancid body was a complete mystery, but humanity had been the one quality Hank lacked since losing his children.

"Oh, you two would be in buckets if it weren't for that Big'un. It was watching us, from the shadows. It thought it was being clever, but I knew it was there."

As if waiting for a dramatic entrance the Alpha suddenly appeared, roaring across the roof top, having scaled the side of the building like King Kong. Darren and the Patterson's hearts collectively sank as the Alpha smashed through the stack of kindling. Sending debris, Stan and Red hurtling through the air like skittles.

Darren braced for impact as the Big'un slammed into him with tremendous force, crushing him against the cold brick wall. In an instant the Alpha slashed his throat, sending a mist of blood into the air.

It was strange, Darren knew he was badly hurt, but he just felt numb. All that effort, getting back to the hotel, hoping Red was okay, all for nothing. He couldn't see a life without his dear friend, so maybe it was for the best he moved on from this world.

After all what good is a bodyguard without someone to protect.

The Alpha had made good on its promise, returning in numbers, with its gathering following into battle like loyal dogs.

Darren's vision was still severely blurred, saving him from the sight of the now present twenty strong gathering looming over him, smacking their decaying lips with anticipation. It had been far too long since they had eaten a fresh one and they were going to savour every single bite.

They descended upon Darren like a pack of vicious hyenas, tearing and clawing away delicious meaty chunks, swallowing him piece by piece.

Darren's triumphant comeback was over just as quickly as it had begun.

High above the gruesome scene, the Isaac thing silently circled the night sky before descending towards the roof ledge below.

The Alpha lifted the netting, allowing the grotesque bird to take its rightful place on its master's arm. The Alpha tossed his new pet a scrap of fresh Darren meat, Isaac catching it in its twisted, blackened beak.

"More!" it squawked, motioning a bony wing towards Mr Darling's unnaturally twitching corpse.

"Tainted meat" grunted the Alpha, who then viciously kicked Mr Patterson in his side, breaking several of his ribs.

Mrs Patterson lost consciousness, saving her from the despair of seeing her friend treated with such disregard. One by one the gathering finished their Darren meal, and left Mr Darling and the Patterson's to turn as commanded by their leader. Hank watched on from the far corner, as the gathering of Big'uns passed by like he wasn't even there.

Then like the clans, once led by William Wallace, charged into the hotel ready for battle. Their monstrous footsteps booming down the narrow stairwell, on the hunt for juicier, untainted, live humans.

Now on his lonesome, Hank surveyed the path of destruction laid before him. Unlike the Alpha, he wouldn't leave Mr Darling to turn, as it would just lead to extra competition. Crawling over to Mr Darling, Hank took hold of his lolloping head and twisted with all his might.

There was a disgusting, cracking and snapping sound as his body went limp. That should have been the end of it, but Hank kept twisting with every ounce of unnatural strength in his contaminated body. With a squelch and a splatter, Mr Darlings head came free of his body, tumbling to the floor.

Hank then took the largest and sturdiest piece of kindling he could find, inserting the sharpest end into the base of Mr Darlings skull. Raising the severed head high into the air, as the last traces of his humanity disappeared into the ether. The Patterson's began to display the tell-tale twitch of the dead, but luckily for them, and their still attached heads. Hank had made the final transition from man to zombie.

He passed by the Scottish couple, just as the Gathering of Big'uns had passed him prior. Heading through the smashed fire exit, ready to join his new family, whether they wanted him to, or not.

The residents were now down to seven.

Bad Habits

"Slow down! Take a breath, everything will be alright."

"What part of my husband is dead wasn't clear to you?"

Elinor looked Mrs Darling square in the eyes, but there wasn't anything she could say that would make the situation any better.

"Well, both of you come in here and shut the door quick!" Lewis ordered as Avril shuffled in, shutting the door behind her."

They brought with them a sense of despair that quickly filled the room like a balloon. It was almost palpable, hanging in the air, surrounding them. Mrs Darling went into the bathroom and inspected herself in the mirror. She had been caught in the frenzied splatter, looking like a Jackson Pollock painting, with blood red and bile black thrown against the canvas that was her face. The hotels water supply had stopped running long ago, but Lewis had gathered enough rainwater in one of the communal buckets to have a wash each day.

She took a flannel, dipping it into the bucket, the water was a few days old and microscopic insects had laid their larvae at the surface. But that didn't matter, Mrs Darling just wanted to be clean, she couldn't bear the thought of her husbands' blood being all over her. She quietly cleaned herself, all the while trying to keep a stiff upper lip, but that didn't stop the awful sobbing that came naturally to the surface.

Avril on the other hand had sat herself down at the foot of the double bed, staring at her own reflection in the mirror opposite.

Lewis sat on the sofa with the boys and with shifting eyes instructed Elinor to see if Avril was okay.

Avril jolted as Elinor gently placed a hand on her shoulder. "Shh, it's okay, you're safe now."

A single tear rolled down Avril's cheek.

"We're not safe, just trapped."

Elinor looked back at Lewis who gave an encouraging nod.

"Hey, listen we have a way out of here, a car, that's how Lewis and the boys got here. They want to leave and take us with them, what do you think?"

Avril simply shrugged and displayed a dismissive expression. "It won't matter, nothing matters anymore, not without her, this is all I have left of her now.

She leant forward and pulled out the blood-stained note from her back pocket, opening it. Scanning the first few lines only to be disappointed.

"Well, I guess I don't even have that, it's for you."

She held out the note for a confused Elinor who took the piece of paper, quickly realising it was from Alec of all people.

"This is from Alec? Was he on the roof with you?"

Avril shook her head.

Elinor began to silently read the note, with a feeling of concern rising from the pit of her stomach.

"My dearest Elinor, I hope this letter somehow finds its way to you, sorry I'm not able to give it to you in person. I hate to sound soppy but if you are reading this, then you're probably aware that I'm dead (sorry if you didn't know that bit.) It's okay though, just know that I went out on my own terms, well kind of.

Anyway, I just wanted you to know something, something that I could never find the courage to tell you in person, don't worry its nothing romantic.

Sorry I'm rambling, bad habits I suppose.

You, Elinor, are the very best of all of us, kind, sweet and a dab hand when it comes to looking after yourself. If there were more people like you in the world, then maybe we wouldn't be in this mess.

I might be a relic from a time long forgotten, but I know something special when I see it, and you my dear, are something very special indeed.

Tell the others I'm sorry if I was too harsh on them, I just wanted them to live their best lives (Red taught me that saying, I dunno if I used it right.)

I wanted them to have the skills to not just survive, but thrive.

But I need you to do me a favour, get as far away from here as possible, and take them kids and Lewis with you. They need looking after, plus he seems like a good bloke (Just don't tell him I said that!)

Under The Managers rule the hotel won't last much longer, you see, them things have their eyes on this place.

The big one that got into the hotel today, well there's bloody loads of them. They live just opposite from us, sorry I didn't say anything about them before, he made me keep quiet about the whole thing.

There are a few bits in my room you can have, hidden under the bed, but everything you need to get on the road is stashed in conference room four.

Just kick the door in and take it all when the time comes. The Manager won't be able to stop all of you, then you can take that sporty blue car Lewis and the boys arrived in (yes, I know about it, you could hear the bloody thing coming from miles away!)

Anyway, I guess that's me done.

Thank you for bringing a little bit of sunshine into this horrid place, I will miss you Elinor.

All the best,

Alec."

A steady stream of tears began to flow down Elinor's cheeks as she silently wept. There had been so much death in the hotel lately, but she honestly thought Alec would outlast them all. In her mind he was like the love child of Alan Titchmarsh and the Terminator.

Able to grow fresh edible fruit and vegetables in the most baren of lands and seemingly indestructible. But he was gone, and that broke Elinor's heart.

"We're leaving, all of us, right now!" she said, clenching her fists and standing to attention.

"But we just got here!" said Tom who wasn't great at reading a room, throwing himself back onto the bed as melodramatically as possible.

Lewis rolled his eyes and nudged Tom "behave yourself!"

Then walked over to Elinor, taking the letter and scanned the first few lines before Elinor snatched it back.

"That's private" she snapped. The room fell deathly silent.

"I'm sorry, I didn't mean to snap at you, it's just time to go, okay?"

Lewis put an arm around her and gently brushed the hair out of her eyes. "It's okay and you're right, it's time to go.

Mrs Darling emerged from the bathroom looking considerably cleaner, although she was still visibly shaking.

"We off then? Bout bloody time, I've had it with The Manager and his rubbish. Her false posh accent completely vanished, now replaced with something that would have fit in nicely with the cast of The Only Way is Essex.

The corners of Avril's lips reluctantly curled up, quickly becoming a wide, toothy smile, leading to a full-blown belly laugh.

"I knew that accent wasn't for real! I just knew it!"

Much like the virus, the laughter was most contagious and one by one the group broke out into fits of hysterical laughter, even Mrs darling couldn't help but find the comment funny. That was until the inevitable tears started to flow once more, this time from both Mrs Darling, Avril and Elinor.

The trio shuffled their feet uncomfortably, unsure of where to look or what to say.

Thankfully, Elinor broke the tension.

"We need to go to conference room four, then we're out of here."

Lewis looked at her with a perplexed expression but trusted there must have been a good reason.

"Okay, we will go there first then get on the road, we just need to pack our stuff here and then."

"No, leave it all behind, everything we need is in that room. We get in, take it and go, understood?" said Elinor, interrupting Lewis.

"I have my own stash, but it won't be enough for all of us, so it has to be conference room four, understood!"

No one dared argue with a tearful lady, they all knew better than that.

"Okay, but we do need one thing," said Lewis.

"Yeah? What is it?" asked Mrs Darling.

"Boys, get Sebastian the duck.

The Gathering

Hank brandished Mr Darlings head on a stick, causing the Gathering of Big'uns to momentarily stop on the staircase. It was an impressive sight to behold, never had they seen someone so recently turned with such an intense thirst for human flesh.

Even the Alpha was taken back as Hank parted the gathering like the red sea, flanked by his ghostly companions. Hank grunted with a splutter, commanding the gathering of Big'uns to follow him in what appeared to be a change of management at the hotel.

"Do it, kill em all" ordered the female ghoul.

"Yeah, they kept all the good stuff for themselves and made you do all the work" added the boy.

Hank didn't need telling twice as he lured the Big'uns down the stairwell with Mr Darlings head, like a carrot on as tick.

With utter disregard for the do not disturb signs, they reached the first floor, alerting the residents in room one-oh-five to their presence.

Upon hearing the commotion, the remaining residents made a discreet exit. Lewis leading the way, the boys behind him and the ladies at the rear.

Sebastian the duck was now safely tucked inside Lewis's coat pocket. On his way out, Martin made sure to grab the second most valuable item in the hotel, the mobile phone and charger.

Elinor was the last out of the room, shutting the door gently as possible, but the click of the latch was enough to reach the putrid ear canals of the Gathering. The gathering increased their speed, bounding along just in time to see the back of Elinor sprinting ahead of them.

The chase was on.

Hank didn't have the speed the Big'uns possessed, as they roared into action, like greyhounds on a racetrack. They smashed and crashed into the white corridor walls, knocking large chunks out of the plaster. Leaving thick marks, from floor to ceiling, pushing and shoving each other, bottlenecking the corridor, turning into a dirty mass of claws and teeth.

The residents reached the ground floor in record time, racing towards the closed doors of conference room four. One by one slamming into the unforgiving wood, alerting The Manager who had locked himself inside after fleeing the rooftop.

For once the room wasn't vibrating with the sounds of eighties mega hits, instead it was unnervingly quiet.

"Let us in! let us in!" Lewis cried out as the gathering of Big'uns reached the ground floor. But there was no answer.

"Kick the doors in, come on! Quickly!" Commanded Elinor as all six of them proceeded to boot and shoulder-barge the doors as hard as they possibly could.

The door frame groaned under their weight, as suddenly the double doors flew open, causing the residents to topple into the room with a collective "oomph."

Just as the trio had arrived at the hotel, The Manager pulled them over the threshold to safety once more. "Hurry up! Come on get inside!"

His eyes darted between the residents and the looming gathering, calculating if there was enough time to save them all before barricading the doors shut. But there wasn't.

Everyone managed to get into the room except for Mrs Darling, as the doors slammed directly shut in her face.

Immediately the gathering descended upon her, tearing into her flesh with their bony fingers and jagged teeth. Blood sprayed in every direction as Mrs Darling took a sharp breath inward, unable to scream, unable to comprehend the sheer volume of pain. She silently passed on from this life to the next, as the Gathering huddled around her, stripping flesh from bone.

At the back of the huddle, stood the Alpha, adorned with the Isaac thing atop of its shoulder and Hank, still brandishing Mr Darlings head.

The two of them watched the gathering feast, as growls and wet chomps echoed from wall to wall. Both displaying twisted gapped tooth smiles.

"You killed her! you monster! How could you!" screamed Avril.

"I'm sorry, but we had to close the door, or we would all be dead right now" exclaimed The Manager.

There was no time to argue, as the residents looked around for anything to barricade the door with. They quickly realised they were surrounded by stacks of tinned food, water, charcoal, medical supplies, all sequestered within The Managers personal fortress of solitude.

But all the multi packs of chocolate bars in the world were no match for the Big'uns, who were now lunging at the door with brute force, having made quick work of Mrs Darling.

"So, are we all in agreement, that if we survive, we kill The Manager?" Said Lewis as he threw a pack of Turkish Delight at him.

"Fine by me," said Elinor.

"And me" added Martin, not wanting to be left out of the conversation.

The Manager pretended not to hear the snide comments and frantically piled up his ill-gotten goods. The Big'uns pounded on the door with all their might, with Hank watching on with a sense of self satisfaction. Never in his wildest dreams did he imagine being a zombie could feel so good.

Connecting words together in his mind like a jumbled-up puzzle, he bellowed at his new companions. "Open it!"

The door began to buckle and splinter, small pieces at first, but gradually the frame crumbled.

"Yes, yes! tear it down."

Hank's eyes were practically bulging out of his head with wicked glee.

The Isaac thing wasn't as accepting as the rest of the gathering when it came to their newest addition, looking down his beak at Hank.

It stretched out its wings and positioned itself, ready to take flight. Isaac could only accept one master and it certainly wouldn't be the likes of Hank. It let out a ferocious screech, suddenly swooping for Hank's vulnerable looking head.

But Hank had already noticed the demon bird looking at him sideways, preparing himself for the inevitable assault. Taking a classic fencing stance, he rammed Mr Darlings head straight into the putrid heart of Isaac, in an explosion of bones and tattered feathers.

Isaac fell to the floor, stunned, semi-conscious as Hank raised his diabolical mallet high into the air. Bringing it crashing down with all his undead might. Both Mr Darling's and Isaacs skulls shattered as they violently collided.

In an instant the formally brilliant bird was no more.

The Alpha, stood there in stunned silence, unable to process what this former human had done to its loyal companion.

It did several double takes before the severity of the situation dawned upon it. In a matter of minutes, this head wielding zombie had not only infiltrated its gathering but also killed Isaac. The Alpha roared and ungodly roar, louder and more aggressive than ever before.

This gained the full attention of the gathering!

As frightening as the roar sounded, it was a welcome reprieve for the residents who continued stacking various goods. The gathering surrounded The Alpha and Hank, circling them to ensure neither of them could pass. The contested leadership needed to be resolved before going any further, much like Thunderdome, two would enter, but only one could leave.

The two sized each other up, one scrawny, dripping with blood. The other larger, unnatural looking with entrails adorning its thick neck. Rather sportingly Hank threw down his weapon, opting to use his two hands to take down his adversary. Much to the Alphas delight, as it was still severely wounded from the previous clash with those pesky humans.

"Mine!" growled the Alpha, pointing an elongated finger to the gathering.

Hank smirked "Don't think so."

The two formally living creatures, threw themselves at each other, in a violent whirlwind of punches and kicks. Bouncing back and forth as the gathering kept them within the confines of the circle, their rancid eyes fixated by the confrontation.

Hank was surprisingly holding his own against the Alpha, taking it down with a leg sweep, like an MMA fighter. The Alpha crashed to the floor with an almighty thud, crushing the Isaac thing even more. It let out a high-pitched whimper like a dog with an injured paw, as the bird's ribcage exploded, embedding deep within the Alpha's back.

The Alpha tried to stand, but its legs were limp as noodles, forcing it to crawl away. Like a shark circling its prey, Hank smelt blood from his injured foe. There was a clear winner here, as one by one the rest of the gathering knelt for their new leader. The Alpha was spent, left with no choice but to conceded defeat.

All that time, studying the humans, keeping the gathering safe, amounted to nothing.

"Kill me" it whispered.

Bits of Mrs Patterson blocked Hank's ear canals, making him hard of hearing, as he leant in closer to hear the Alphas dying words.

This was all the opportunity the Alpha needed as it struck Hank square on the jaw, sending him flying across the room, smashing through the circle and into a wall. He lay there for a moment, woozy and stunned as the Alpha cackled with joy.

The gathering watched on, unsure of what to do, they needed someone that could do all their thinking for them. But it looked like the newest member was still in with a chance, as he propped himself up against the wall. Now wielding the bloody stump on a stick that was once Mr Darlings head.

Hank staggered over to the Alpha, who somehow was back on its feet, like Rocky Balboa, asking for one more round.

Their eyes met, as suddenly all those foggy memories came rushing back to the Alpha, like someone had shone a light in the darkness. His name was Alan and he had been a footballer, a really good one. He used to play for Swindon Town, travelling from place to place for matches.

He loved being on the pitch, the cheer of the crowd, the smell of the grass. In fact, the only thing he loved more than football was his wife, Becky.

As the memories flowed through Alans infected mind, Hank dealt a barrage of hideous blows to his face. The first with enough force to knock his one good eye clean from its socket, across the hallway, blinding him. A second, third and fourth blow followed in quick succession. Each time caving in Alan's face deeper and deeper until he was reduced to a twitching pile of mush and maggots.

Hank had won.

Hank's lungs worked overtime, collecting precious breath as the gathering rose from their knelt positions, accepting their new leader.

Wasting no time Hank pointed towards conference room, instructing his new minions to finish the job. Not needing to be told twice, the gathering threw themselves at the locked doors, forcing them open with a colossal shove.

Mountains of charcoal and marshmallow showered the room, sending a combination of soot and sugar into the air. The undead charged blindly into the room, ripping and tearing anything apart in their path. Hank held back, waiting for those delightful screams, but to his dismay, they never came.

Sticking a finger in his ear, removing a piece of Mrs Patterson, which tasted delicious. He listened intently, but still there was nothing, not a peep.

As the air cleared, it quickly became apparent the humans had fled.

Not to worry though, as even in his formally living state, Hank knew the hotel better than anyone. They wouldn't get far, and when he caught up with them, there would be a feast the likes of which the hotel had never seen before.

The residents were down to six.

All panic And No Disco

Panting, sweating, the residents arrived back at the reception area having, snuck through the rear exit and made their way back to the front. The main doors to the hotel had been ripped off their hinges, laying strewn on the concrete steps. Several Big'uns must have entered this way, as well as having scaled the building. In a true display of intelligence, using the time-tested divide and conquer strategy.

Even the trusty metal railing had buckled under the sheer force from the gathering of Big'uns. The Residents could have made a break for it, but they needed those supplies. As they simply couldn't afford to escape with nothing more than the clothes on their backs.

The plan was to sneak back in while the Big'uns were quarrelling, giving them just enough time to hide in one of the ground floor bedrooms. Hopefully, they would lose their sent and get bored, moving on. But that was unlikely.

To make matters worse, another gathering had descended upon the hotel, drawn in by the commotion on the rooftop. These zombies may not have been agile as the Big'uns, but they had strength in numbers, looking to have two hundred plus within their ranks.

Lewis froze to the spot, uncertain as what to do, as the massive gathering flooded through the hotel like a raging river. It didn't take long for the front runners to notice the residents tiptoeing through the reception area, as they stared down their potential fresh meals.

Lewis took a short, sharp breath, to get rid of a stitch that was starting to spread down his side, before shoving the boys onward.

"Come on, come on, hurry!" he called out.

As both The Manager and Avril closely followed behind.

They passed through some double doors, into a long dark corridor, moving towards the closest bedroom. But it was locked with a heavy-duty looking padlock, forcing them to move onto the next room. This was also locked, as was the next one and the one after that.

It suddenly dawned on Lewis, that Hank still had the keys to every door on his formally living person.

They were trapped.

"What are we going to do?" asked Tom.

But Lewis didn't have an answer.

Behind them was a massive gathering, and ahead of them, beyond the next set of doors were the Big'uns. They were lambs, being led to the slaughter.

Perhaps it would have been best to just leave after all.

"Wait, where is Elinor?" asked Avril?

A quick head count revealed there was only five of them, meaning she had either been caught in the zombie tsunami, or had made a run for it. Although disappointed, Lewis hoped it was the latter.

"Dad? could I please see Sebastian again?" Asked Martin.

Lewis looked down at his little outstretched hand, wondering why he would choose this moment to ask such a thing.

"Please? He makes me happy, and if I'm going to die, I want to die happy."

Lewis burst into tears, realising it was his son's final request.

"Of course you can see him." He said, reaching into his jacket pocket only to find the rainbow wigged duck was missing.

"He's not here I'm afraid, the cheeky duck must have flown away."

Martin sighed, "never mind, at least I have you two."

Lewis knelt and embraced his two sons, holding them tightly.

The Manager and Avril clasped hands, readying themselves for the end.

The doors behind them began to rattle, as the undeniable stink of the gathering filled the air around them. The doors at the other end of the corridor were suddenly flung open.

It was the Big'uns.

Much like the Patterson's and Darren before them, their hearts sank upon seeing the rancid gathering.

"I am so sorry, I got you all into this mess, you didn't deserve any of this," sobbed the Manager. "It was my duty to ensure the comfort of all my guests, and I failed you.

Lewis looked him square in the eye "Hey, you tried your best, that's all anyone can ask for."

The Manager half-heartedly smiled and nodded at Lewis.

"Well it appears I have one final duty to carry out."

"Hey, listen, don't do anything foolish. We have a car, big enough for all of us, Maybe we can still get out of this, together" pleaded Lewis.

"A car? Is that how you got here?" questioned The Manager.

Lewis just nodded.

"I had a car once myself; I loved that thing. It was blue, gleaming and the engine, wow what a ferocious noise it made. It was American, totally impractical on English roads and forever breaking down, but still, I loved it."

With the dead closing in, now may not have been the ideal time to bond over car, But a perplexed Lewis had to ask The Manager if they were talking about the very same car.

"Wait, was it a Dodge Avenger?"

The Manager paused for a moment and smiled, "I see you have met her. Could you do me a favour please, give her a fresh coat of wax, that's the very least she deserves."

Lewis nodded, practically reading The Managers mind, knowing this would be the last time they would ever speak.

"Hey, I have to ask you, what is your name? I mean really what is it?"

"Check the guest book, it's the first entry." He said, passing him a black leather-bound book that had somehow been concealed upon his person.

Lewis took hold of the book, wanting to flick through the pages then and there. But for the time being, decided it best to tuck it safely underneath his coat.

The Manager extended his hand to Lewis, the two shaking hands with a firm, manly embrace.

"We didn't shake hands when first met did we. Not to be rude but you really did need a good wash."

Lewis chuckled as a lump formed in his throat.

"Oh and I believe this belongs to you" said the Manager, handing a yellow plastic bath duck, complete with sunglasses over to Martin, which he happily accepted.

"Thank you for everything" said Lewis, trying his best to hold back his emotions.

The Manager nodded, patted both Tom and Martin on the shoulders. Not realising just how sore they still were from Hanks previous grasp.

He then gave Avril a kiss on the cheek, bidding her farewell, as she embraced him deeply.

"Thank you, it was nice while it lasted" she said.

The Manger simply nodded, then turned to face the gathering of Big'uns.

"Now then gentlemen, you don't appear to have a reservation, so I will have to ask you to leave!"

Before anyone could stop him, The Manager ran towards the gathering of Big'uns, leaping at them with every ounce of strength he could muster.

Hitting them with such force, they toppled over like dominos, allowing the doors to close behind them. It happened all so quickly, and yet seemed to happen in slow motion as the four remaining residents embraced one another, mourning their fallen colleague.

They didn't blame The Manager for the mess they were in, in fact Lewis admired him. He just wanted to create a place with a semblance of normality, in a world that was anything but.

The Managers final act was to give his guests a few more minutes of precious life.

Avril, Lewis and the boys wept, holding onto one another. Waiting for their horrid fate, as the doors behind them trembled, buckled and blew of their hinges.

The two hundred plus gathering had arrived.

But they were acting odd, distracted even, looking back over their shoulders towards something. Over the dull roar of the gathering was another sound, louder and more powerful than all of them combined.

It was Dreadnought!

The reception exploded into a shower of tables, zombie parts and carrots, as Dreadnought began to do donuts, running down anything in its path. Lewis picked the boys up by the scruff of their coats and firmly nudged Avril to move. They quickly zig-zagged in and out of the distracted gathering, darting towards the blue blur that was the mighty Dodge.

Rubber squealed against the marble floor as the car continued to mow down the gathering one by one. Limbs were crushed, organs imploded, blood splattered across every surface.

All that work carrying the garden down from the rooftop had amounted to nothing. As raised plant beds exploded, scattering soil and human waste across the room. Whether it was the driver's intention or not, several lit candles and a lantern were caught in the collision. Sending them hurtling, igniting splintered wood and tablecloths in an instant. Unless the fire brigade were on route, then it appeared that Red and Zombie Stan would have their cremation after all.

Dazed and disoriented, the gathering had been reduced to only a few stumbling, rotten zombies. All of whom were beyond skinny, weather worn creatures, desperate for a morsel of living flesh.

Dreadnoughts tyres smoked and screamed, as the vehicle came to an abrupt halt, long enough for Lewis to see the driver. It was Elinor.

"Need a ride?" she called out as the car made painful clunking noises, las it may fall to pieces at any moment.

The residents made a break for it, frantically pulling at the passenger doors. Elinor had never done donuts in a car before, but she had seen enough trashy films to get the idea, plus it felt really cool. The tiled floor was now slick with a rancid smelling trail of mush, causing Avril to lose her footing as she ran over.

She caught herself on the front passenger side door, causing it to slam shut with a metallic bang. But managed to trap her fingers in the process, breaking several of them with a singular snap.

Avril screamed in pain and rightfully so, as Lewis quickly opened the door, freeing her.

Her fingers were bent at horrid looking angles, red and swelling at a frightening rate.

She whimpered and staggered backwards.

"Avril just get in the car ,and we can take a look" Lewis called out.

But the pain was too intense, dulling her senses, clouding her thoughts and judgement. Avril began to bawl, as a steady stream of tears flowed from her bloodshot eyes.

This was all the opportunity the dead needed, as two gaunt looking zombies descended upon her. They had been beautiful women in their former lives, tall and slender, still sporting fancy looking jewellery and leopard skin crop tops.

They could have been sisters, an unspoken bond keeping them together even in death.

Simultaneously they sank their jagged teeth into Avril, one deep into her neck and the other tearing an ear off with a singular bite.

Avril went limp, her eyes rolling back into her head as she passed out from the pain. Blood splattered against the car, coating the windows, causing the passengers to shriek with horror.

Lewis reached out instinctively, but was held back.

"It's too late, she's gone, please just get back in the car" pleaded Elinor as she held on to Lewis's coat. She was heartbroken, but there was no other choice.

Lewis looked around; the flames had spread at an alarming rate, as the gathering recuperated. Several zombies were now ablaze themselves, spreading fire deeper into the hotel.

It was officially time to check out.

Reluctantly Lewis climbed back into the car, checking the back seats, as both Tom and Martin stared right back at him blankly.

The colour drained from their faces, Martin looking rather sick, but doing his very best to not let it get the best of him.

Lewis gave a nod to Elinor, "thank you for coming back for us."

"Well, I couldn't leave these two behind now could I" she said with a sly wink towards the boys.

She was visibly shaken herself, but tried her best to keep their minds off the horrific situation.

"What do you think about Elinor's driving skills?" questioned Lewis, only to be met with silence.

The boys feared that if they opened their mouths to respond, the contents of their stomachs may make an unwanted reappearance.

Lewis locked the doors and leant over, giving Elinor a kiss on the cheek. She smirked and paused despite the looming danger surrounding them.

"Wanna try that again?" she asked.

It took Lewis far too long to work out what Elinor meant. Luckily for him, she filled in the blanks, leaning in for a passionate kiss. The kiss was slow and firm, but also highly inappropriate given the circumstances. Both Tom and Martin recoiled in disgust, not sure if the sight of their dad kissing Elinor was worse than dealing with the undead.

"Stop it, I already feel sick" quipped Tom, killing any romance.

"Shut up and put your seat belts on!" ordered Elinor as she hit the accelerator with full force, sending the quartet hurtling towards the exit.

Lewis and the boys quicky did as they were told, strapping in for the ride. Dreadnought collided with several zombies for good measure, sending a grotesque spray of body parts and organs across the windscreen.

Momentarily blinded, Elinor pulled back at the windscreen wipers, as the nozzles offered a mere morsel of fluid. Clearing just enough of the windscreen to see a Big'un hurling a piece of metal fencing at them like a javelin.

Glass shattered into a thousand pieces, as the railing pierced dreadnaughts windscreen, causing Elinor to wildly veer out of control, as she desperately avoided being run through herself.

Dreadnought lived up to its name, as it crashed into the wall, dealing more damage to the hotel than it had taken. The noise from the crash was thunderous, echoing throughout the town centre.

The four passengers jolted violently, leaving them semi-conscious as the wall collapsed in front of them, clattering against the car bonnet.

The once pristine brickwork gave way, causing a strong gust of wind to roll through the hotel like an invisible wave. Kicking up all manner of dust and debris with considerable force.

Dazed and in considerable pain, Lewis tried to shake the cobwebs loose. His entire left side instantly felt bruised as he struggled to turn around, checking on the boys.

"You two okay?"

Martin looked to be drifting in and out of consciousness. He was getting hurt far too often for Lewis's liking. Tom on the other hand looked to have a broken nose, as blood began to trickle down his face.

"I saved it dad!"

Tom had shielded the precious phone, even at the cost of his own wellbeing.

"Well, as long as the phone is alright, that's the main thing I suppose."

Lewis tried to laugh it off, but quickly stopped as even the slightest chuckle caused immense pain.

Elinor was slumped back in the driver's seat, unconscious, as he gently checked her over. But couldn't see anything immediately life threatening.

Pain radiated throughout Lewis's entire body, but it was up to him to get everyone to safety. The seatbelt and his joints clicked at the same time as he freed himself, turning to help the boys.

Martin, still dazed, muttered something to himself, whilst Tom had already undone his seatbelt and was facing out of the rear window.

Tom trembled with fear, but was unable to look away.

"Dad we really need to go."

The gathering of Big'uns had returned, lit by the glow of ever spreading flames. Covered in a mixture of Mrs Darling and the Manager's blood, now being led by the infamous Zombie Hank.

"You, ain't, leaving!" bellowed Hank, as he weaved words together within his infected brain. Rallying the others into action.

The front end of the car penetrated the wall of the reception area, straight into a ground floor bedroom. Lewis forced open the passenger side door with his one good arm and climbed out.

"We have to go!"

From here they could crawl into the bedroom, putting a crumbling mess of concrete between them and the dead. Tom shook his brother, which probably wasn't the best idea, but given the circumstance, could be forgiven.

"Five more minutes please mum." Martin moaned as he stirred back into life.

For a fleeting moment, he was back in his own bed, toasty and warm, his mum gently waking him up for another day of school with his friends. But suddenly he was dragged back to reality, his friends were gone, as was his mum. Martin began to cry, which Lewis mistook for pain, but he just felt incredibly sad.

He had been through so much in his young life and things only seemed to be getting worse.

Tom unclipped his brother's seatbelt and shoved him into their dads' waiting arms.

"I will get us out of this, you just need to be brave for me!" Lewis called out.

Martin was sick of being brave, sometimes he just wanted to cry, was that such a big deal he wondered.

Tom climbed over to the front seat, following his family, bricks continuing to clunk against the car bonnet, scaring him half to death.

Time was truly against them, as the gathering were now pulling at the exposed bricks, picking them out one by one like a twisted game of Jenga.

The boys crawled through the small opening into the bedroom, as Lewis removed the keys, unclipped Elinor's seat belt and lifted her to safety with a pained grunt.

The four of them were back in one of the familiar bedrooms, this one previously belonging to Hank who happened to be blind, which was an awful mess.

Discarded food packets and empty water bottles cluttered every surface. Dirty clothes covered every inch of the floor.

At that moment Lewis realised that no one had been caring for Blind Hank, leaving him to his own devices. But perhaps he had been too proud, or simply embarrassed to ask for help. Either way, it was no wonder as to why Blind Hanks disappearance was easily dismissed after the Alphas initial attack.

"Boys, follow me and keep close!"

They did as instructed, sticking to their dad like glue, running towards the door, putting as much space between them and the gathering as possible. But in the chaos no one had noticed the distinctive smell of petrol, as a shard of thick metal had punctured Dreadnought's fuel line.

Then, a Big'un swiftly burst through the crumbling wall, like it were crepe paper. It leapt onto the car roof, leaving two deep indents, as the wall gave way completely behind it. Inadvertently entombing its gathering, in its wake and partially bringing down the room above.

The Big'un roared as the residents tried to exit the room, but panicked as the door became stuck on an old cereal box.

Working together, Lewis and the boys un-stuck the door and made a hasty retreat.

Then, just like an unstoppable force meeting an immovable object, a singular flame inched forward, through the wall opening . Fire and fuel making their way towards each other, as the remaining residents ran to the upper floor.

"Keep up you two, we have to keep going!"

"But, but, when we get there, what do we do?" asked a breathless Tom.

"We can climb down a drainpipe, I did it once before"

Lewis wasn't sure if this was the best plan of action, but they were plumb out of options, with the Big'un advancing towards them.

There was also one other problem that was becoming more evident the longer Lewis held Elinor. He was starting to lose all the strength and feeling in his left arm. His shoulder was dislocated, hanging limp at his side, sending shooting pains all the way down to his toes.

It was then, the three sides of the fire triangle met, heat, fuel and oxygen, combined as dreadnaught erupted with a deafening explosion. Glass shattered, furniture vaporised, walls and ceilings tore asunder in the blink of an eye.

The mass gathering were all but wiped out in an instant.

It appeared that Lewis would be unable to grant The Managers final request, of providing Dreadnought with a coat of wax after all.

Lewis and the boys stumbled, losing their footing as the floor beneath their very feet, violently shook. Persevering, Lewis carried a still unconscious Elinor with one arm, all the way to the rooftop in record time. As the boys tried their best to close the damaged fire exit door behind them.

The splintered wooden frame barely held on, as they kicked and pushed the misshapen door back into place. But it was like putting a square peg into a round hole, no longer lining up.

They stopped, exasperated, it would have to do.

The scene upon arrival was simply awful, blood, innards and body parts laid strewn in every direction. Rabid pigeons were tangled up in the netting, no longer content with their strips of finger meat. Mr Darlings headless and battered body, lay spread out in the middle of the rooftop, displayed like a crime scene. Darren's remains were simply beyond recognition, whilst the Patterson's lay motionless, with various chunks missing. Lewis covered his mouth, stifling a sicking feeling, bubbling up from the pit of his stomach, but it was no use. The contents of this morning's breakfast, which mostly consisted of spam, passed his lips. Clearing an impressive distance.

Exhausted, Lewis wiped the sweat from his brow, his lungs working hard to pull oxygen into his body. Then he saw it, his eyes widened with panic as he realised the danger he was about to be in.

A familiar silhouette emerged from the far shadows.

"Nasty cut kiddo."

Lewis's heart sank. "Hank please, the hotel is on fire!"

Unlike Zombie Stan and Zombie Ollie, Hank couldn't be reasoned with, or domesticated.

But the last thing Lewis wanted to do was to fight.

No longer able to feel his left arm, he desperately wanted to put Elinor down. But now wasn't the time to show any signs of weakness.

Hank grunted and bore his teeth like a wild animal, ready for the kill

"Oh, sod this!"

Lewis cried out, as he kicked Hank square in the chest, causing him to slip and fall into the remains of the Patterson's.

Gently, Lewis laid Elinor down, as Tom and Martin stood behind him.

"Hang on boys, I just need to have a word with your teacher."

Hank was now back on his feet, twitching unnaturally, ready to finish off the troublesome humans. Lewis and Hank glared at each other, neither of them wanting to go down without a fight.

It was clear only one of them would be leaving the Hotel, as living and dead were about to clash in an epic battle of survival.

Without warning, the fire exit door flew off its hinges, as the remaining Big'un crashed through, with blood lust. It lunged for the delicious humans as the trio closed their eyes tightly and braced for the worst.

But Hank swiftly stepped in between the attacker, and its potential victims, momentarily saving them from a gruesome fate.

"Not yours!" Hank snarled at his new lacky.

The Big'un looked at him with utter distain, but with the Alpha gone, it quickly conceded, opting instead to block the only means of escape.

After all, once Hank was done, it could still suck the marrow from their tender bones.

Lewis opened his eyes, expecting the sight of the Big'un to have descended upon them.

But instead, was greeted by the wide toothed, smirking Hank, beckoning him to a duel of undead fisticuffs. Standing himself up, keeping a now stirring Elinor and the boys behind him.

Lewis readied for the fight of his life.

The residents were down to four.

Check Out Time

Thick smoke bellowed from the ground floor windows, penetrating the senses, making it difficult to separate the living from the dead.

Hank lunged from one direction, while the Big'un stood fast. Lewis kicked up a large pile of ash, straight into Hanks eyes, blinding him.

Had there been more time, perhaps Lewis could have appreciated the irony of this Hank being blinded. But now was not the time for such things.

The Big'un didn't seem to appreciate the humans underhanded actions and lunged towards Lewis, its claws fully extended, ready for the kill.

Quickly, Lewis side stepped as the Big'un collided with a stumbling Hank, the ash cloud giving him a slight advantage.

They roared and hissed, quickly regrouping, Hank wiping the muck from his pus-filled eyes, sprinting towards his prey. Lewis ran across the rooftop, drawing them away from the others, but the living impaired were much faster than him.

The Big'un bounced around wildly, sprinting on all fours, like an unholy dog. Hot on his heels, the Big'un leapt, arms outstretched, swiping with its claws, only to miss at the last possible second, as Lewis commando rolled out of harm's way.

He slipped in what he hoped to be a dirty puddle, only to realise it was a sickening combination of the former resident's blood and innards. But there was no time to dwell, as Lewis bounced back to his feet like a boxer, displaying fancy footwork.

But he knew he couldn't outrun them forever.

Darting towards the intertwined mess of kindling, Zombie Stan and Red's lifeless bodies, he grabbed the largest and most sturdy looking piece of wood.

"Come on! All I need is one good shot!" he cried out, swinging his make-shift weapon.

But deep down he knew he was exhausted, running on fumes.

Hank and the Big'un, managed to bypass Lewis's weapon, slamming Lewis into the wall with such force that it popped his shoulder back into the socket.

"Arrggghh!" he screamed as pain shot throughout his entire body.

But then, suddenly he felt better, now able to move is digits without wincing.

Fending off the Big'un with the piece of wood, and Hank with his foot. Angling the wood just underneath the snapping and snarling Big'uns chin, forcing it upwards with all his might.

With a vulgar cracking sound, Lewis forced the Big'uns head so far back, that it snapped its spinal cord. In an instant the Big'un dropped to the floor, motionless, killing it for a second time.

Stunned, Hank watched his new lacky pass on, in front of his rancid eyes.

Lewis couldn't afford to hesitate though and quickly swung again, this time striking Hank in the side of his face with a sickening thwack. Rendering him unconscious, as he crumpled to the floor.

But there was no rest for the wicked, as something grabbed his shoulder. In a flash Lewis turned and clobbered the figure, this time catching them with the blunt end of the wood.

It was Martin.

"Oh my god, I'm so sorry, are you alright?"

Martin rocked backwards, before stopping himself from toppling over. This time there weren't any tears, just a stern expression directed towards his dad.

"Really? Again!"

"I'm so sorry, this is getting to be a bad habit." Lewis quickly checked Martin over, his cheek was most definitely going to bruise again.

"What are you doing? It isn't safe."

Instead of answering, Martin simply stepped aside, revealing a very cross looking Elinor. She looked awful, displaying multiple cuts of varying sizes and depths all over her body. Her lovely, flowing locks, now filled with a mixture of blood and grime. But even so, Lewis couldn't help but think she still looked incredibly beautiful.

If they got out of this situation, he was definitely going to ask her out.

"She woke up, asking for someone called Hugh, she needed help, did I do the right thing?" asked Martin.

Lewis couldn't have been prouder; he had shown such selflessness despite the horrid situation.

He knelt and embraced his two sons, never wanting to let them go, choosing to ignore the dull pain shooting throughout his arm.

If it weren't for the quickly spreading flames engulfing the hotel, and the fact the dead wanted to feast upon them, it would have been the perfect family moment.

"You did amazingly, thank you! Now come on its time to get the hell out of here!"

This was easier said than done, as hundreds more zombies had surrounded the hotel, drawn in by the light, like moths to a flame.

Even up on the roof, the sounds of crackling, fizzing and popping could be heard, as the fire consumed everything in its wake. Not only would Lewis have to navigate the route between the battlefield of strewn body parts, but he would also have to support Elinor's weight.

"Come on now, easy does it" said Lewis as he gently placed Elinor's arm around himself.

Had the circumstances allowed it, Lewis would have placed his hands over the boy's eyes, leading them past what was left of the residents. But unfortunately, Tom and Martin saw every disturbing detail, every splash of blood, every exposed vital organ, which made them feel queasy all over again.

"Dad is that the Patterson's?" asked Martin, unable to pry his gaze away.

"Hey, eyes up yeah? Look at the stars," commanded Lewis. "You see those three stars in a row, well that's Orion's belt."

The boys looked skyward, as prompted.

That was one good thing about the apocalypse, with no light pollution, the night sky lit up, more beautiful and spectacular than ever before.

In an orderly line, they moved to the edge of the roof, that connected with the gym next door. Apart from a singular supply run previously carried out by Darren and Red, the gym had remained empty since Black Sunday.

Checking over his shoulder, Lewis made sure Hank was still out for the count. He lay in a heap, twitching as if being electrocuted over and over.

Hank's skin was turning a deep shade of purple, displaying an unnatural rapid, onset of deep vein thrombosis.

Lewis watched him for as long as possible, until satisfied he wouldn't get up again, more than happy to let the fire finish him off.

"Okay, I'm going to need you to climb over to the other side, just like we did with that fence in the field, do you remember?"

The Boys nodded in unison, Martin holding his sore cheek once again. Lewis had no idea a hematoma could form on that part of the body until now.

"When you get on the other side, I need you to help Elinor over."

She was still drifting in and out of consciousness, terribly confused by everything, once again asking for Hugh.

"Please, I have to get back to Hugh, we are going to the cinema later, I can't be late."

Lewis looked at her with a concerned expression. There was no telling just how hurt she really was, or even if she would make it. But they couldn't leave her, not after everything she had done for them.

Tom lifted the netting, suddenly aware of the infected pigeons still tangled above them. They squawked furiously, frustrated, unable to strip the juicy flesh from the human's bones.

Tom no longer looked at Orion's belt, but instead for anything circling the night sky.

He leapt across to the adjacent rooftop, his feet disappearing in deep pile of ash. In doing so the mobile phone fell from his trouser pocket, clattering towards Lewis.

Tom sighed, but fully understood the urgency of the situation, as he extended his hand towards his little brother.

"Okay now you."

"Okay, just don't let me slip."

"I won't, just come on, we have to go!"

Martin did as his older brother instructed, leaping into his arms.

"Dad, the phone, can you get it please?"

It didn't even matter to him that the charger was long gone, now in the charred remains of Dreadnaught. To Martin this was the one ring, his precious, the hotel ablaze was Mount doom and he wouldn't allow it to be cast into the fires.

"Elinor first, then the phone yeah?" said Lewis with a hint of annoyance.

Cradling her head, Lewis passed her over to the boys, both holding their arms wide, outstretched, at the ready. But they hadn't quite braced themselves for her weight, letting Elinor flump to the floor, disappearing into the dark pile of ash.

"Oh god, is she alright?" Lewis asked, already knowing the answer.

"Sorry, are you okay?" asked Tom as Elinor sat bolt upright.
Now covered from head to toe in black ash, making the whites of her eyes more prominent, like sparkling diamonds amongst charcoal.

"Are we out of that bloody hotel yet?" exclaimed Elinor.

"Technically yes" but we still have to get the hell out of here, can you walk?" questioned Lewis.

Elinor nodded, pulling herself up with the boys help. Her legs felt weak, as she momentarily stumbled around like a new-born deer.

Tom and Martin were at the ready, their hands outstretched, not wanting her to fall for a second time.

"Okay, climb over and let's go" a now steady Elinor said to Lewis who was more than happy to join her on the other side.

Placing both of his palms down flat, against the ledge, readying to hoist himself over, Lewis suddenly realised the back of his head felt warm and wet.

Tom, Martin and Elinor looked at him with shocked expressions, their hands firmly clasped over their mouths.

The boys began to cry, silent tears, both glued to the spot.

"Hey what's wrong?" asked Lewis, but no one responded.

Placing a hand on the back of his head, confirmed it was indeed warm and wet. Lewis looked to the skies above, expecting to see an infected pigeon had defecated on him, but there was nothing.

Slowly he brought his hand to his face, confirming the worst-case scenario, it was blood, a lot of blood. Lewis turned around to see what had caused the wound, but already knew the answer.

It was Hank.

The boys and Elinor could clearly see the deep and jagged laceration, as blood poured freely down the back of Lewis's head and neck.

Hank had managed to get back to his feet, undetected just long enough to stick the pesky human with a sharp piece of plastic, from The Managers music player.

Now standing there with a look of pure glee upon his face, truly proud of himself.

"Raspberry-ripple" grunted Hank.

"It's alright boys, just know whatever happens, that I will always be with you. Keeping you both safe."

The boys and Elinor wept as Lewis suddenly threw himself at Hank, taking him down to the ground like a UFC fighter.

They watched on in silent horror, as living and dead clashed, dealing blow after sickening blow to one another. For a moment it appeared that Lewis had the upper hand, straddling Hank and repeatedly slamming the back of his head against the rooftop.

But Hank just smirked, with wide eyes, looking wildly at Lewis.

"Come on get up, you can beat him!" called out the ghostly girl.

"Yeah finish him off" added the ghostly boy as Hank suddenly threw Lewis off, clear across the rooftop.

Hank leapt to his feet, truly enjoying himself, violently kicking Lewis in the side, breaking two of his ribs in the process.

Lewis fell to the floor, motionless. He was done for.

Hank walked over to his downed opponent, placing a dirty black boot upon his chest. Hank then looked upwards to the heavens and roared a positively mighty roar, declaring victory. He then knelt down, taking in a delicious deep whiff of his next meal.

Lewis gasped for breath, he wanted to call out to his boys and Elinor, he wanted to tell them to run, but was simply unable to.

Now flanked by the ghostly figures of his children, Hank smacked his decaying tongue against his lips.

"Hey there kiddo's, who's hungry?"

He then bore his teeth, ready to sink them deep into Lewis's carotid artery.

Lewis closed his eyes tight, bracing himself for the worst, when suddenly Hank recoiled in anguish.

There was a light, so positively bright that it blinded all before it. It was being directed by Martin as he shined fifty lumens of piercing light, from the mobile phones torch, directly into Hanks eyes.

Hank fell backwards, squealing with pain as the virus had rotted away the membranes to his retinas. No longer able to process bright lights such as these.

Quick as a flash, Tom and Elinor dragged Lewis away, all the while Martin stood over the formally, formidable Hank.

"I knew this thing would come in handy!" Exclaimed Martin.

The phone only held a mere fifteen percent charge, but it was more than enough to keep Hank downed once aimed in his direction.

With Lewis now safely tucked to one side, Tom stood over him protectively. Elinor quickly took hold of Alex's old toolbox. It was a heavy, rusted old thing. The once red paint chipping away at the corners and around the handles,. Still it did its job.

With a variety of tools inside, it had a considerable amount of weight to it, enough to finish off Hank once and for all.

Elinor held it tightly by the handles, then stood on both of Hank's two hand's, pinning him down. Hank writhed around, thrashing out his legs, like a wild animal caught in a snare trap.

But unable to get away.

"Kill the light, I want this bastard to see what's coming" Elinor instructed Martin.

Martin did has he was asked, then quickly ran over to be with his family.

No longer blinded, Hank oddly calmed down, now motionless as he and Elinor locked eyes, almost as if accepting his fate.

Elinor raised the old toolbox, high into the air.

"Mr Two-Hands, The Manager will see you now."

She cried out, as she brought it down, with every ounce of strength that she could possibly muster.

The toolbox clattered against Hank's skull, as several tools spilled out. But Hank was still alive, gargling upon his own congealed blood. Elinor raised the toolbox high again, bringing it crashing down with a splatter.

Again and again, over and over, Elinor rammed the toolbox into Hank's now misshapen face. Blunt metal meeting flesh in a horrid symphony of clanks and squelches.

Elinor stopped her onslaught, just long enough for life to flicker once more, within Hank's eyes. As he looked past her, towards his children.

He grunted and sputtered, trying to form words, that ultimately failed to come.

But in his warped mind, he was speaking his dying words, as clear as day.

"It's alright kiddo's, just know whatever happens, that I will always be with you. Keeping you safe."

Then, with one final breath, just like that, Hank was no more.

The Way To Mordor

It wasn't easy, but one by one the quartet had climbed down the drainpipe to the ground below. The gathering had scattered, realising fire and zombies made for poor bedfellows. Making it easy enough to fall back to a safe distance. Finally, the remaining residents were safe.

The flames tore through the hotel, making it clear, that it was truly lost, leaving them to ponder, just what to do next.

"Thank you for saving me, all of you" said Lewis who was still woozy and beat up.

Thankfully, with a bit of applied pressure, the blood flow seemed to be stopping, but he would need stitches and antibiotics sooner rather than later.

"You still want to go north?" Lewis asked Elinor, who paused for a moment, giving it some thought.

"Well, we can go anywhere we want right?"

Lewis nodded in agreement.

"Well, we could go north, or" Elinor knelt to Tom and Martin's level, placing a hand on each of their still tender shoulders.

"We could borrow a rocket ship and go to a place on one of Pluto's moons, called Mordor. Alec once told me all about it."

"Tell me boys do you know the way to Mordor?"

Lewis chuckled, whilst the boys didn't quite get the reference.

How about you Lewis, where would you like to go most in the whole wide world?" she asked.

"Well, I always wanted to travel to Wells in Somerset, see all the iconic locations from that film, Hot Fuzz. Maybe go to the shop and get a Cornetto."

Elinor smiled, it wasn't the answer she was expecting, but had to admit, it did sound fun.

How about you two, where do you fancy going?" Lewis asked the boys.

Tom and Martin took a moment to confer, whispering with each other.

"Well." said Tom. "We always liked our holidays at Butlins, they were fun and the thing is, Martin doesn't really remember them, so."

Lewis knelt and smiled at his boys, looking up at Elinor, who simply nodded with approval, as tears filled her eyes.

"I think that's the best idea anyone of us has had in ages."

The boys beamed and instantly grew excited, as Lewis stood up and took Elinor by the hand.

"Plenty of tall fences, fresh air and right by the ocean, "What's not to like."

There be would a lot of ground to cover, between here and Butlins. They would face many dangers along the way. From both the living and the dead.

But as long as they were together, they stood a chance, and that's all anyone in this world could ask for.

"Hey, do you still have the guest book?" asked Tom?

Lewis placed a hand inside his coat, mindful of his tender ribs, and removed the slender, black book.

"Cool, we need to keep it, that way, we are bringing them all with us, do you know what I mean?" asked Tom.

"I know exactly what you mean" said Lewis proudly.

"Wherever we go, the residents will always be with us. We will keep their memories alive."

Elinor gently nudged Lewis. "We better get going, every formally living person in Stevenage must be on their way here by now."

Lewis sighed. "Yeah, your right, but before we go, shall we see what the Manager's real name was? He said it was in this book."

Elinor and the boys smiled, and leant in as Lewis opened the book for all to see. The wildfires of the hotel cast flickering, manic shadows, that made for difficult reading.

Together, the quartet read aloud, like an apocalyptic karaoke session.

"Welcome to the Holiday Inn Express, Stevenage, haven for all."

"Ask for The Manager."

Guest Book

Welcome to the Holiday Inn Express, Stevenage, haven for all. Ask for The Manager.

Please sign in the guest book, and feel free to add any suggestions to help us make your stay more enjoyable

1) Date unknown.

Suggestion: People are free to be who they want to be at this hotel. Names and past lives no longer matter. From this day fourth I will simply be known, as The Manager.

2) Alec Newgrange - Date?

Suggestion: There is a B&Q not far from here, it could be worth a look for gardening equipment.

3) Hank Allen - Date, not a clue.

Suggestion: We need to do something about those two Zombies, the ones in smart suits. I think I have an idea.

4) Stan and Ollie – Date unknown.

Suggestion: Grrr, argh. Just kidding, these two can't write, but are a welcome addition to our little venture! – The Manager.

5) Reginald and Petunia Barclay – Date, August? Maybe September.

Suggestion: Perhaps some local advertising is needed?

6) Tara North – Date, who knows?

Suggestion: Head to the Isle of Wight, I heard its meant to be safe there!

7) Hank Marshall – Date, I wish I knew!

Suggestion: Set up a classroom and maybe decorate a little. Give us something pleasant to look at while we are here.

8) Elinor - Date, not known.

Suggestion: Nothing for the moment, I am just grateful to be safe, for now.

9) Margery Churchill – Date, I'm not sure, sorry.

Suggestion: The hotel needs a proud motto, something along the lines of; Stop, look and listen.

Although I think that might also be the green cross code. I will come back to this later.

10) Darren - Date, Must be late Winter, maybe January if I had to guess.

Suggestion: No suggestions just yet, but I'm happy to pitch in around here.

11) Matt Bentley - Date, ???

Suggestion: I thought I saw some people in the hotel opposite, so will see who has more to offer.

13) Mr and Mrs Patterson - Date, Ney thanks,' we are married.

Suggestion: Lovely place you have here, but Twelve herrings an' a bagpipe make a rebellion.

13) Avril and Red – Date, the doomsday clock, reads quarter past midnight.

Suggestion: Don't display peoples last names, it's a breach of GDPR.

14) Lewis, Tom and Martin O'Conner – Date, our lucky day!

Suggestion: We are happy to contribute in any way possible. Thank you for taking us in, we look forward to the future, whatever it may hold.

15) The manager - Date, it appears to be the finale of the hotel.

Suggestion: Just my sincere thanks to all the residents of the hotel. For a short time you helped me achieve something special, that I truly thought to be impossible.

Your kindness and warmth shall remain with me, until my final moments. I in turn hope that you enjoyed your time here, not just as residents, but as a family.

Wherever life takes you, remember to support and love each other.

But most importantly.

Please, do enjoy your stay.

The Manager

Acknowledgements

This book is the result of over two years of procrastination!
Some days, thousands of words were written. Other days were spent getting the margins just right.
Perhaps I am the true zombie, excuse me, I mean formally living.

But here we are, one finished book, and the sequel already in the pipeline. Which is further than I ever expected to get.

From the first word, to the very last, there have been a LOT of changes in my life.

Changing jobs in the middle of a global pandemic, moved in with my Fiancée. Helped to plan our wedding and took care of my family as best possible, who are a constant source of inspiration.

Thank you to Emma who read my story, despite me constantly changing it, and asking her to start over again.

I do appreciate it and I am truly lucky to have you in my life.

You won't get to read my wedding speech though, you will have to endure that on the day!

Also thank you to my two quirky boys, for allowing me to portray them in a not-so-great light. Your peculiar habits have given me years of writing fuel, and I look forward to your teenage years!

Finally thank you to anyone who reads this.

In all honesty I'm not sure how well this story will do, but if you make it past the opening line, then I truly appreciate it.

I was once told by the author Mick Foley (New York Times bestseller) to write about what I know, and write from the heart.

And so I did just that.

Having grown up in Stevenage, which allowed me to use it as a setting for my story. Hopefully, the residents of Stevenage find this tale interesting!

I hope you all enjoy my odd little story, and I look forward to welcoming you to the next entry in the OutBreak series.

The OutBreak Resort

Lee David Congerton

Printed in Great Britain
by Amazon

10395312R00115